THE KEY
OF IDELISIA

THE KEY OF IDELISIA

BOOK ONE OF
The Key Trilogy

WRITTEN BY
Sharon A. Roe

ILLUSTRATED BY
Quillan H. Roe
Onnee and Elspeth Roe

FIRELACE EDITIONS

Published by FireLace Editions

ISBN 978-1-7331138-0-9

First Printing 2019

Printed by Bookmobile, Minneapolis, MN
Book design by Sarah Miner
Cover illustration by Quillan H. Roe

For Stephen,
with all my love

Author's Note

This book is all about family, whether the family we're born into or the one we choose. The author has chosen three gifted artists to create the artwork that enlivens the text. The discerning reader will notice three different styles represented. Most of the art is by Quillan, son of the author Sharon. A few renderings are by Onnee and Elspeth, daughters of Quillan and granddaughters of Sharon. Each one's vision creates and illuminates the world of Idelisia in their own particular way.

List of Characters and Settings with Pronunciation Guide and Gaelic Derivations

OELSA: *OHL-suh* · Main character; 12-year-old girl

DAHVI: *Dah-vee* · "beloved" · Oelsa's father

FIAL: *FEE-uh* · "generous, honorable" · Leader of the ravens; shape-shifter

BIAB: *BIBE* (from Gaelic *Badb*) · "battle raven, war goddess, inspirational" · Raven; companion to Fial

BRAND'OO: *Bran-DYOO* · "black raven" · Raven who leads the search for Oelsa; rescues G.W. and Samson from the WilderOnes

ANVYARTACH: *AN-vyar-tock* (Gaelic *Ainbheartach*) · "doer of evil deeds" · Shadow Lord; seeks revenge

MANGRED: *MAN-grehd* · Anvyartach's second-in-command; sent to kidnap Dahvi

UHLAK: *OO-lawk* (Gaelic *Uallachan*) · "little, proud arrogant one" · Second soldier sent to find Dahvi; steals Hunt Disc

G. W. L'AEGE a.k.a. Grammy Wizard L'Aege: *LEG* · Old wizardess; Oelsa's grandmother

SAMSON: Orange cat; companion to G.W.; carries feline magic

WILDERONES: Bear-like invaders from the northland

KELLACH: *KELL-ock* · "war, strife" · Leader of the WilderOnes

FAWKEN: *FAW-kin* (from Gaelic *Fachtna*) · "malicious, hostile" · A WilderOne

SKAWHOK: *SKAW-hokh* (from Gaelic *Scathach*) · "shadowy, frightening" · A WilderOne

ARDREAS: *ARE-dray-us* (from Gaelic *Aindreas*) · "manly" · A GreatOak; forest caretaker; helps Oelsa search for Dahvi; captured by beetles

FESTIE: *FESS-tee* · "malicious" · Beetle prince

PROMELIOUS: *pro-ME-LEE-us* · Beetles' captured beast; covered with metallic, silver blades; G.W. befriends him

FIREICE: Powerful weapon created by Anvyartach; black ooze that devours all life energy and raw emotions

VELVET: Mangred's whip

IDELISIA: *EE-del-EE-see-uh* · "bountiful, idyll" · The homeland

FINNIS FEWS: from two Celtic words for "woods or forest" · The great forest that covers much of Idelisia

TIRVAR: *TEER-varv* · "the dead country" · Anvyartach's homeland in the northern part of Idelisia

ADARE: *uh-DARE* · "oak tree grove" · Home of the GreatOak Clan

ONEHOME: Home of G.W. and Samson

TALLACH: *TAL-akh* (from Gaelic *Taichleach*) · "peacemaking" · Ancient tree; protector of others in Ring of Ancients

NUALA NI L'AEGE: *NOO-la* · "fair shoulders" · G.W.'s many greats Grandmother, First Creator; protected Idelisia from Anvyartach

TOWER OF KEDRIC: Mythical tower from First Age; helped First Creators defeat Anvyartach

SHEELIN LAKE: *SHEE-lin* · "lake of the fairies" Great Mirror Lake · Eastern lake in Idelisia; Tower of Kedric rests beneath its surface

THE MAP OF IDELISIA

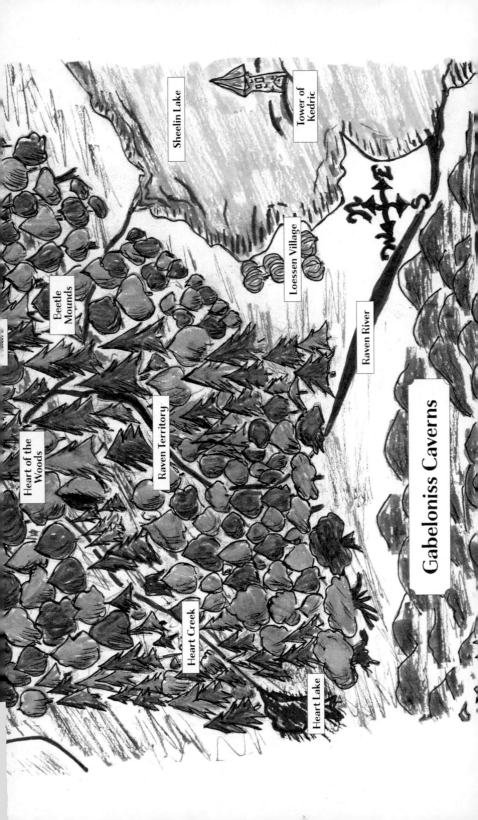

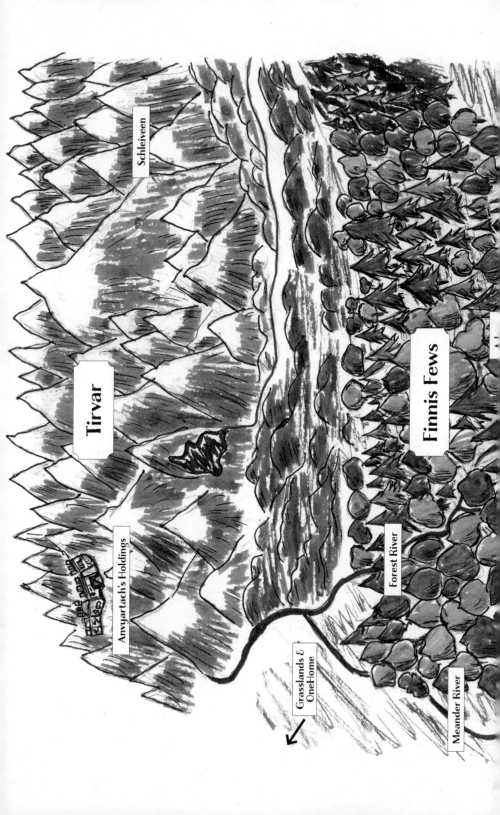

THE KEY
OF IDELISIA

1

DARKNESS AT THE EDGE of the great forest Finnis Fews crept back as the morning sun inched upward. In the little cottage at the Heart of the Woods, twelve-year-old Oelsa slept peacefully under her faded quilt, her unruly auburn hair bunched across her forehead. The sounds of her father, Dahvi, splitting logs drifted into her sleep. Oelsa's dreams carried her along a pleasant, peaceful stream like the one near their cottage. The abrupt silence of the birds alerted her first. When shouts and thuds reached into her dreams, Oelsa leapt from her bed.

Dahvi yelled, "Take your hands off me, you stupid oaf!"

She bolted for the door and jumped from the porch. She landed running, her bare feet slapping against the dirt path that led around the cottage. Her only thought was, *Keep him safe.*

As she rounded the corner, a blinding explosion knocked Oelsa off her feet. Sulphurous smoke enveloped her. Her ears rang, deafening her momentarily. Oelsa staggered to her feet and swept her arms through the thick smoke. The sound of a heavy object being dragged from the woodlot penetrated the fog.

"FATHER! WHERE ARE YOU?"

Smoke drifted into the forest. Oelsa stared around the woodlot. The carnage stunned her. Her father's axe lay twisted on the ground, iron bent like soft dough, its wooden handle splintered as if blasted by lightning. His homespun shirt lay torn and trampled in the dirt. Heavy boots had gouged the ground and a deep gash disappeared into the woods. A dark pool near the chopping block caught her eye. She dabbed her finger into it. "Blood."

Oelsa spun in circles. "Bring him back!"

A faint sound caught her attention. She stopped twirling and glared at her surroundings. Nothing. Trembling with shock, Oelsa realized words were in her head: *Run away, Oelsa, or they'll get you too!*

The unexpected warning doubled her over. She dropped to her knees and threw up. "Come back, Father! Don't leave me here alone."

Shivering with fear and disbelief, Oelsa tried to make sense of what her eyes were telling her. In a matter of seconds, the security she had known living in the Heart of the Woods with her father was destroyed. The protective shield that had kept them safe her entire life was shattered and Oelsa's world changed forever.

Overhead, a large raven circled and dropped unexpectedly onto the chopping block: *Pruk-pruk-pruk!* His glossy feathers glistened in the morning light. When Oelsa didn't respond, he called again: *Prruk-prruk-prruk! Toc-toc-toc!*

The sound grated on Oelsa's ears as she watched the raven dance on the stump. He continued a long series of trills and croaks followed by growls and yips and jumped down. As he hopped toward her, a small, yellow stone with a hole in its center dropped from his back where it had nestled among the thick feathers. He used his heavy, black beak to push it toward her.

Oelsa reached out and grasped the stone.

"Don't worry, Little One."

Oelsa leapt to her feet as though she had been shocked and

dropped the stone. The only two beings in the woodlot were the girl and the bird.

Keeping her hazel eyes on the raven, Oelsa leaned over and retrieved the stone. When the bird strutted toward her, she pulled back but continued to clutch the stone.

"Your father's life is in danger."

Oelsa's eyes widened.

The raven continued. "This little stone helps you understand my language. I imagine all you've heard up to now was *pruk-pruk-pruk*." He chortled as though it amused him to hear his own bird sounds the way a human might.

Frowning, she looked at the bird, then looked at the stone in her hand, and looked again at the large raven. "How can I understand you? You're a bird."

The raven's neck feathers ruffled. "I apologize for startling you. Let me introduce myself." The commanding bird stretched his wings to their full four-foot span, inclined his head with the grace of a king, and bowed.

"I am called Fial, son of Fearghus, son of Finnbar. My family goes back to the Dark Time, and beyond. We are known for our peculiar ability with languages as well as for our exceptionally glossy feathers." His eyes sparkled with pride.

Oelsa opened her mouth and blurted, "I can't be talking with you. You're a bird." As she pointed at Fial, she dropped the yellow stone.

Toc-toc-toc! Fial hopped toward the yellow stone and pecked at it with his thick, polished beak.

Oelsa stared hard at the bird before she retrieved the stone.

"Better," Fial sighed. "Try not to drop it again. It is rather rare."

Oelsa struggled with the reality that she could understand this bird.

The raven looked directly into Oelsa's eyes. "Something dark and unnatural has entered Finnis Fews. Your father's disappearance is no doubt connected to this, Oelsa."

Not pausing to wonder how this bird knew her name, Oelsa retorted, "You mean his kidnapping! It has to be a kidnapping. Look at all this damage." She gestured toward the pool of blood. "My father wouldn't simply disappear," she said, and added under her breath, ". . . and leave me all alone."

Swallowing hard to keep back tears, Oelsa asked, "Who could possibly want to harm my father?"

Fial strutted back and forth, considering his words. "He knows something, I'd guess. Something of great importance. Otherwise they wouldn't bother to take him alive."

"Alive? But he has to be alive, doesn't he?" Oelsa's face reddened.

The raven paced around the chopping block. "He's in no mortal danger yet, not until—"

"Until what?" His answer wasn't the comfort Oelsa wanted.

"Well, I mean to say . . ." Fial had to tell her something, but how much? She'd had such a shock already. "Did your father ever tell you about your world, child?"

"My world? Yes, of course." Memories of her father carrying her through the woods, naming the plants and animals, and explaining their dependence on one another flooded her mind. Oelsa looked at the ravaged woodlot and shook her head. "He always said our home at the Heart of the Woods was safe."

She sighed deeply. The morning's events destroyed that notion. "Father said Idelisia was beautiful and someday we'd explore the rest of it."

Her frown deepened. "I can't make any sense of this, Fial. How will I ever find my father?" In her thoughts she added, *I'm only twelve years old.*

Fial's reply startled her. "You're no longer a child, Oelsa. And, yes, I can read your thoughts, especially when you leave them so open."

Instantly, all the fear and uncertainty of the morning ignited into a ball of fury within Oelsa. Eyes narrowed and lips pressed together,

Oelsa raised her arm to throw the yellow stone at Fial's head. "Who gave you permission to pry into my thoughts, ever?"

Fial hopped back and flapped his outstretched wings.

The movement startled Oelsa and she looked at her clenched fist. "Oh," she moaned as she sank to the ground and burst into tears.

Fial touched her shoulder with his left wing. "There, there, child. It's been a difficult morning."

When Oelsa lifted her head and wiped away her tears, Fial said, "You still have the stone. Where would we be without it?"

Oelsa stared at the raven. He just said "we."

All that happened that morning rushed through her—the fight and her father's disappearance, the raven and his yellow stone, the fact that she was able to talk to and understand a bird who had arrived at the worst possible time in her life. All these events had to mean something.

Lifting her shoulders, Oelsa faced Fial. "Well, raven, what do we do now?"

2

IN THE FAR NORTH OF IDELISIA, in the place called Tirvar, the Shadow Lord's castle crouched on a rocky knob of land, its turrets sharply silhouetted against the sinking sun. The stronghold of the Shadow Lord, whose name was Anvyartach, was made from jagged stones blasted from the surrounding mountains. Since his return to this inhospitable land, the snow and ice had intensified, creeping farther south, forcing Tirvar's creatures to flee or perish.

Countless rooms and a maze of hallways coiled through the bleak fortress. Window slits filtered the dim light. Little heat penetrated the thick walls. At one end of the Great Hall, Anvyartach slumped on the cold throne carved from a massive piece of granite. He rested his head on his bony hand. "How long has it been, Mangred, since I sent you to find the woodcutter?"

As he leaned against the throne's chilly arm, Anvyartach remembered the day he'd ordered his strongest and most trusted henchman on this mission. "Bring the woodcutter to me, Mangred. He has the secret. I'm sure of it!"

Kneeling in front of his Master, Mangred bowed his head. Through sheer will he kept his trembling legs from betraying his fear.

"Don't fail me, Mangred. You remember what happened to the last one who failed me, don't you?"

"Yes, Master. You can count on me." Mangred half stood, backed away, and hurried from the Great Hall.

Several days had passed since Mangred's departure, and Anvyartach's thin patience was stretched to breaking. A large, glass orb sat next to the throne. He lifted it, held the opaque ball in front of his eyes, and shook it violently. "Worthless. How can I follow Mangred's progress if this wretched thing remains cloudy?" Red blotches began to spread over his skin as he wrestled the glass ball into its holder.

Frustration fed the rising fury that filled Anvyartach's every waking moment. "Those wretches will pay for what they did to me." He rose from the cold throne and reached for the large mirror sitting to the right of it. "Who is this weakling in the mirror?"

The last time he'd been whole and complete had been eons ago, but Anvyartach remembered every second of the ordeal. The words of banishment and dissolution of his body and soul, pronounced by all the First Creators and led by that wretched, old witch were as fresh in his mind today as they were all those eons ago. "Banish me, will you? Blast my atoms into the far reaches of the universe, expecting I'd never return? Well, I am *back*. You'll soon wish you and all your progeny had never been born!"

His hand shook so hard he nearly lost control of the mirror, but with supreme effort he managed to set it down without breaking. "Dark times," he snarled. "But I've shown them. My powers are mightier than anything they ever imagined."

At first, there had been no thought, only a cold, disembodied nothingness, absolute oblivion. Inexplicably, however, minuscule pricks of awareness were followed by the faintest wakefulness as his individual atoms cried out for one another across the vast reaches of

the cosmos. One by one, in excruciatingly slow degrees, each atom found each microscopic other. The evil within them yearned across the universe, hungering, longing, aching, drawn irresistibly closer and closer until they found one another and bonded, piece by piece. One moment nothing; the next—alive!

The memory still thrilled Anvyartach. That it had taken eons for this miraculous reuniting was inconsequential. It happened and he was back, ready to crush those who had dared to oppose his powers. The woodcutter held information essential for the next step, and Anvyartach would rip it from him.

"Where are you, Mangred?" Shadowy slaves scurried along the walls and crept out of sight.

Grasping the edges of the heavy cloak he wore night and day, Anvyartach lurched upright. His left foot unexpectedly shot out to the side, tripping him, and he fell onto his face at the bottom of the throne. The Shadow Lord howled and flailed as he tried to extricate himself from the enormous cape tangled around his legs. Before he could get his balance, his right leg spasmed, throwing him sideways. He landed hard on his elbows and slumped on his side. "NO!" he shrieked as he wrestled with his uncooperative body. "HELP!"

Slaves sidled cautiously toward their flailing Master, as terrified of his uncontrolled movements as his unbridled rage. One tugged on the heavy cloak, untangling it from his body. Under its folds the man was still forming. At times like these, when none of the parts worked together, helping him was even more dangerous.

"Get away from me!" Anvyartach meant to slap the one who dared touch his arm, but his hand bounced against his own chest and nearly knocked him over again. "Leave me be. I can do this myself!" Anger made the coordination of all his parts resist even more.

One slave cautiously crawled toward the windmilling Master. "Please relax. This is a slow and unpredictable process. Your banishment was so very long, and your new body needs time to re-form."

Hearing those soothing words, Anvyartach did relax; his breathing slowed, and he managed to pull himself into a sitting position. When the slave reached out to help him stand, Anvyartach lashed out, sending the poor man sprawling. "Never remind me of that horror."

Anvyartach couldn't predict when he would lose control of some part of his newly forming body, but he would not be mocked by some sniveling slave.

"Bring me the glass orb." Pulling himself upright, he placed one foot onto the first stone step. When no new spasm occurred, he stepped up again and again until he could collapse onto the throne. Breathing hard, the Shadow Lord masked his humiliation. "You're leaving greasy fingerprints all over it. No wonder it won't show me where Mangred is."

Fortunately for Anvyartach, his brain had been one of the first parts of his body to find its myriad components. His ability to think clearly improved daily. But the skull housing the brain, and the face that covered the skull, were still works in progress. One eye worked, but the other tended to veer to the outside corner of the socket. His lips quivered uncontrollably at times, and the muscles in his cheeks would droop without warning.

All the muscles in his body and the nervous system that connected them to the brain were new, but wrong connections had occurred. This was such an aggravation that Anvyartach seethed every waking moment.

As his body calmed, Anvyartach slumped on his throne and ruminated about his plan for revenge. *I must get my hands on the woodcutter before he reveals his secret to anyone else. He's the only one who knows the whereabouts of the Key, and without it, I will never control Idelisia. I must know what the woodcutter knows.*

Somewhere in the middle of Finnis Fews, Mangred and the dozen men he'd ordered to accompany him on this mission trudged wearily through the endless tangles of branches. Mangred's thoughts returned to Anvyartach. Chills ran down his spine as he recalled the terrors produced by the Shadow Lord's uncontrolled rages.

I don't know why you do anything or when your magic will flatten me. You said you wanted the man because the man has answers. But answers to what? Could it have something to do with a Key?

Mangred had overheard Anvyartach ranting about a Key several times. "I have to find that beautiful Key, the one with a golden haft encrusted with rubies and diamonds and emeralds." Anvyartach almost drooled as he described it. "And when I hold that Key, I will be Idelisia's Supreme Ruler."

Once, Mangred had dared to ask, "What Key are you talking about, Master?"

The response was swift and vicious. The blow sent him reeling across the room. "It's *my* Key. You'll never hold that precious Key. Never!"

The memory haunted Mangred's thoughts as he pushed through the pathless forest.

Anvyartach chanted spell after spell until, at last, the glass orb cleared. When he found Mangred and his men pushing through Finnis Fews, he spluttered, "You haven't made any progress at all." He shook the orb violently. "I can't bear to watch another second of your deliberate slowness."

Anvyartach hurled the glass orb at the nearest slave who managed to catch it before it fell and broke. The slave slipped the precious orb into a dark-blue, velvet bag and tightened the gold cords.

"I need that woodcutter, Mangred. I need him now!"

Mangred watched the twelve men, who he chose for their sheer brute strength and lack of intelligence, as they pushed through the tangled trees. His own strength outmatched any of theirs, and he towered well over the tallest one. His six-foot-six-inch frame bulged with muscles. His black, leather vest fit snuggly over his rough, woolen shirt. His heavy boots were soaked with mud from the long, bewildering trek through Finnis Fews. Everything he wore, in fact, was stained with mud by this time.

As they slogged through the forest, only Mangred's hot temper and the sharp bite of Velvet, his braided whip, kept the men from running away. Finally, after endless days and frightening nights, they awoke to the smell of wood smoke drifting into their camp.

Mangred sighed. "We've found the woodcutter at last."

Cautioning the men to be quiet, Mangred ordered two of them to fell a large oak while the rest scouted ahead. Flushed with excitement, Mangred signaled his men to follow his lead.

At the first sound of another axe chopping a tree in the nearby woods, the woodcutter paused, his axe poised over his shoulder. Without warning, several brutes rushed forward and wrestled him to the ground.

"Get your hands off me!" Stronger than they expected, Dahvi wrenched free and knocked down several of the attackers with the blunt end of his axe.

Roaring like a maddened bull, Mangred waded into the fight, his powerful fists swinging wildly. Ducking out of his way, Dahvi slowly circled his attacker. Mangred feinted with his left arm, and then surprised Dahvi with a heavy blow from his right. Dahvi's axe flew from his hands.

Wiping blood from his nose, Dahvi searched for the fallen axe. Mangred kicked it out of the way, threw himself at the woodcutter, and grabbed him in a powerful bear hug. The two danced back and forth until Mangred picked Dahvi off his feet and shook him violently. Dizzy from the shaking, Dahvi struggled until he managed to break free of Mangred's iron grip. He feinted to Mangred's left, grabbed his axe, and landed a blow on Mangred's arm.

"Crush him, Mangred! Grind him into the dirt!" Mangred's men circled the woodcutter.

When Mangred charged, Dahvi stepped to the side. He grabbed Mangred by the neck and squeezed.

Gasping for breath, Mangred fumbled for the secret weapon in his vest pocket—a vial filled with a murky potion Anvyartach had given him. When his fingers felt the small bulge, he prised the stopper from the vial, threw the vial's contents into Dahvi's face, and chanted the spell Anvyartach had drilled into him:

> *Hiccius doccius achrra ahg,*
> *janno macka gangrel bav,*
> *ordelf orrah petric*
> *PRAHV!*

Dahvi toppled to the ground.

Panting, Mangred bellowed, "Take him to the log!"

Two soldiers grabbed Dahvi's arms and legs and carried him to the oak. When they dropped his inert body, Mangred shouted:

> *Uumta grati*
> *mota noxi,*
> *Nha,*
> *Bahk,*
> *BLIGE!*

A flash of light blinded everyone for several moments. Thick smoke choked them. When their eyes adjusted, no sign of Dahvi remained. Mangred's mouth gaped, and his thick, black eyebrows were scorched. A drift of gray smoke circled his head.

Mangred's tongue tingled from the strange incantation. His fingertips were singed. Ash smudged his leather tunic.

"Where is he?" gasped one of the ruffians.

Mangred pointed. "In the tree, fool!"

The soldiers stared, aghast, at what was surely an impossible feat. Their captain's new dark powers terrified them even more.

Mangred ordered the men to pick up the log. "Get your backs into it!"

The men stood on either side of the tree trunk, bent down, and tried to lift it to their shoulders. The weight was so great they couldn't budge it, not until Velvet sang over their heads.

"On three!" Mangred bawled. "One. Two. Three!"

Mangred followed his men into the woods, thinking about how he had subdued the woodcutter. "That's the most astonishing thing I've ever done!" he said, laughing as he goaded the men through the trees.

3

MANGRED TOWERED OVER THE SOLDIERS. Velvet whistled over their bent backs. "Get a move on, you slackers." His coarse, black beard bristled. "You don't want to keep the Master waiting, do you?"

The mention of the Shadow Lord terrified the men, and their groans filled the woods as they stumbled on, carrying the log in which the woodcutter was imprisoned. Velvet cracked overhead as they slogged through the tangled undergrowth of Finnis Fews.

Mangred watched the soldiers for any idler. "Get a move on, you lazy dogs!" They weren't progressing fast enough and his thoughts returned to Anvyartach's promised consequences for laggards.

Velvet bit their shoulders. The men cried out and pushed harder. They'd been driven for hours with no rest and no food. One soldier murmured, "We keep going like this, some of us will be dead long before we reach Tirvar."

Velvet snapped over the soldier's head. When he stumbled and fell, the others lurched sideways, regained their balance, and slogged on. Trembling with fear, the cowering soldier staggered after them.

Mangred's black eyes were like flint as he caressed Velvet. "Anyone else want her kiss?"

From inside the log, Dahvi sensed he was being carried, but his perceptions had been dulled too much to know where he was. All he knew was darkness and the overwhelming presence of tree sap. As he rode in this prison, his senses slowly shutting down, he gathered all his remaining energy to send one last desperate warning to Oelsa: *"Run for your life!"*

"Come on, Fial. My father's out there, somewhere, going through who knows what, and we're just standing around." Oelsa's irritation grew as she stomped in front of the raven. "We can't let him disappear and not go after him."

Fial hopped two steps toward the agitated girl, but instead of answering her questions, he said, "The yellow stone needs to rest near your heart. Do you have a ribbon to string through it?"

"What? You're concerned about how I wear the stone?" But Oelsa turned toward the cottage. "Inside. There's ribbon inside."

Before she took two steps, Fial gently pecked her foot and leapt into the air. "Ouch!" She raised her arm and jabbed her finger toward the raven. "Tell me right now who you are and what you're doing in this part of the forest."

From over her head, Fial trilled loudly, and the trees surrounding the woodlot filled with more ravens than she had ever seen. Fial's troop had joined them.

Oelsa stared at the regal birds and tried to count the different kinds. Their black plumage glimmered in the sunlight, some turning iridescent purple while others glowed with an emerald sheen. Each raven, head held high, beak polished, radiated dignity.

Unnerved by their sharp eyes, all of which were trained on her, Oelsa crossed her arms over her chest.

Fial landed on a nearby log. "Remember the yellow stone, Oelsa. Put your hand over it, there, above your heart."

She cupped the stone in her hand and a jumble of thoughts nearly overwhelmed her. She rested two fingers of her right hand on the stone. "I can hear all of them," she whispered, "and they're all wondering why you've called them, Fial. They seem to think you're some kind of magician."

Fial hopped off the log, lifted his wings over his head, and twirled. As he came to rest, he lowered not his wings, but his arms. Standing in front of her was a striking, black-haired man well over six feet tall. Where feathers had been, a voluptuous black robe, embellished with stars and moons that glimmered from its deep folds, flowed from his shoulders. His piercing, black eyes twinkled as he gazed at Oelsa's astonished face.

"They are right, of course."

Oelsa stood transfixed, her eyes and mouth wide open. She tried to speak, but her mouth couldn't form words.

"Think, Oelsa. I can read your thoughts."

"I hate when you do that. Stay out of my head, you, you . . . wizard."

Fial's laughter filled her mind.

A thousand new questions arose, but before she could ask anything, Fial lifted his arms and addressed the congress of ravens.

He's magnificent, Oelsa thought.

"Glorious kinfolk. Thank you for answering my call. The danger I foresaw months ago has moved with surprising swiftness."

Shimmering feathers rustled through the trees accompanied by the soft clacking of beaks. Colors shifted as the ravens' moods swung from surprise to fear and settled into outrage. Fial's words upset his troop, yet Oelsa detected nothing but confidence directed toward their leader.

A bird spoke from the shadows. "Great Fial, how is it you did not see the true nature of this threat?" A stately female whose feathers shifted in the sunlight from black to deep magenta stepped forward so Fial could see who asked this impertinent question.

"Bravely asked, Biab. Do you speak for the others of your clan?"

She held her place, unflinching, even when the others gasped and lowered their eyes.

Undaunted, Biab refused to step back.

Oelsa also trembled as she felt the anger in Fial's mind when he addressed this bold challenge to his authority. This didn't feel like the first confrontation between him and Biab; the tension between them was too intense.

"I will answer your question, Biab, even though you have, again, disregarded our Rules of Respect." Fial's voice was cold. "What is revealed to me, and when, is not under my control. I am simply the conduit. What I've told you is to prepare for an enemy threatening our land. Is this not right?"

Oelsa felt the rush of relief wash over the ravens. "Yes! You've warned us for months." She noticed that Biab had inched a few steps back into the canopy of the oak's foliage, but her eyes remained hot points of ebony. She might be nervous, Oelsa thought, but she wasn't giving in.

Fial's movements were so quick Oelsa almost missed seeing the wand jump into his hand. The ground near Biab was singed and her feathers emitted tiny puffs of smoke. Was this a reprimand or an attempt to silence her?

Speaking as though nothing had happened, Fial continued his address to the ravens. "Let me introduce this girl who has just lost her father." He bowed to Oelsa and asked her to say her name aloud. When she spoke, the ravens' curiosity washed over her.

"Her father is none other than Dahvi the Woodcutter," Fial continued. This time their reactions shocked her.

"*Kek-kek-kek! Cr-r-ruck! Prruk-prruk-prruk!*" Their calls were unmistakably complimentary as they stood tall and lifted their ear feathers. Their *rap-rap-raps* signaled their admiration for her father.

"This girl, Oelsa, has lived all her life in the heart of Finnis Fews, protected and safe. I had hoped she would have more time to grow and learn before she had to take up her mission, but evil has its own timetable."

Mission? Oelsa wondered if the yellow stone was working properly. The magician said she had a mission as though this was common knowledge to all assembled here.

"Fial, what are you saying? I don't have time for a mission. My father is gone, and I have to find him before it's too late." Oelsa folded her arms across her chest, defying anyone who believed she had some mission.

"The time for protecting you from the truth is over, Oelsa." Fial looked into her eyes. "The tale of your life and your mission is long, and we need to move. There will be time to talk as we travel. Perhaps you would like to gather a few things for our journey?"

Without stopping to question Fial's words, Oelsa hurried to the cottage. She dressed in a long green shirt that she belted at her waist, soft brown pants that narrowed at her ankles, warm socks, and a pair of heavy boots. She fastened her gray cloak under her chin, lifted her pack onto her shoulders, and glanced around the beloved cottage.

At the door, Oelsa saw her father's favorite shirt hanging on a hook. She grabbed it, tore a strip from its tail, and slipped it into her pocket. *At least I'll have a small part of you, Father.*

In the woodlot, she stood beside the raven-turned-magician. She stared into the forest, longing to see her father standing there, safe. "Nothing about this morning makes sense, Fial. I don't know why this terrible thing has happened, but I *will* find my father."

Fear and anger combined as her first sob broke free. Fial put his arm around Oelsa's shoulders and pulled her close.

"It's all right, Oelsa. Too much has happened today."

From inside the protection of Fial's cloak, Oelsa wept for all she had lost. Gradually a new understanding rose inside her: *The world I knew yesterday is gone. I am no longer the girl I thought I was.*

Fial watched Oelsa's demeanor change as she swallowed the harsh reality of her new world and her place in it. "You will find your answers, Oelsa." He squeezed her shoulder. "Ready?"

Oelsa nodded, took a deep breath, and stopped dead in her tracks. "Did you hear that?"

Fial shook his head.

The girl stared into the woods. Without warning Oelsa darted away. "Run away. He said, 'run for your life.'"

4

OELSA DASHED FOR THE TREES with Fial right behind her. When he grabbed her, Oelsa screamed and flailed against his arms. "Let me go!"

"Calm down, Oelsa." Fial held her in place. "Who said to run?"

"Father. My father just warned me to run for my life. Didn't you hear him?"

"Your father isn't here, Oelsa." Fial gently drew her back to the woodlot. "Tell me exactly what you think you heard."

Oelsa jerked away from Fial. "I *did* hear him. I can't help it if you're too deaf to hear his warning."

Fial held her shoulders. "Was the voice in your head? Has he spoken to you like this before?"

Oelsa wriggled free. "Yes, of course, in my head." But she stopped. Father had never communicated this way. "I did hear his voice, Fial, but how is that possible?"

"I don't know. What did you notice? Was he angry? Frightened?"

Oelsa frowned as she concentrated. "Muffled. Is that significant?"

Fial's voice was gentle. "Very possibly. What else do you remember?"

She shook her head. "What does it mean, Fial?"

"Do you still want to search for him, Oelsa? I can find you a safe place, and we ravens can look for him."

Oelsa gasped and her face was defiant. "It's my *job* to find Father. I'll go on my own if necessary." She picked up her pack. "I don't understand why any of this has happened, but I'm going. He's out there and he needs me." Without another word, she strode to the edge of the woods and disappeared.

Fial's smile radiated warmth as he watched the girl's straight back. "Wait up! We're coming with you!"

The raven troop lifted out of the trees like a single inky wing and vanished over the thick forest canopy.

After two days traveling with the ravens, Oelsa was more tired than she could ever remember. Fial's conviction they would likely find her father in a day or two had not proven true. Worse, the harder she tried to hear him, the more silence enveloped her.

Fial stood beside the bonfire. The ravens had sheltered in the surrounding evergreens and quickly drifted to sleep. When Fial suggested Oelsa settle under the low-hanging branches of the largest tree, she didn't argue. She pulled out her blanket and fell asleep with her head on her pack.

The shape-shifter settled near the fire. In the morning, they would need a new plan, but for now he allowed himself to relax while keeping a wary eye on his troop.

A short while later, Oelsa awoke. "Did you hear something? I think I heard Father calling me."

Fial continued gazing into the fire. "It's nothing, child. Only a dream." Unconcerned, he rested his chin on his chest and tugged his cloak more tightly around him. Oelsa fell back to sleep.

Several minutes passed before Fial rolled to his feet. Something had disturbed him as well. He listened for suspicious sounds and sniffed the air. A foul odor drifted over the camp.

Glancing at the sleeping girl and at the ravens perched above her, Fial knew his troop would protect the girl if trouble broke into the camp. Fierce Biab, too, would show no mercy to anyone or anything that threatened her clan.

From her perch in the nearest evergreen, Biab watched Fial disappear into the forest. She silently lifted into the air, intent on following the shape-shifter. If he was keeping secrets from the clan, she would soon know them.

Passing soundlessly through the dense woods, Fial scanned the darkness for anything that didn't belong. He didn't know what value Dahvi had for the kidnappers, but his instincts told him it must be connected to the ominous visions he was having of an impenetrable cloud building in the north of Idelisia. It had to be connected to the return of the once-banished Shadow Lord, Anvyartach.

Aware that Biab circled overhead, Fial chuckled and kept moving. *That bird has more spunk than her mother and twice the grit of her grandmother,* he thought, *and they had more than any birds before or since.* Fial slipped behind a tall alder and listened for the crunch of footsteps that would reveal the presence of intruders.

Danger was creeping through the woods. FireIce, the newest creation of the resurrected Shadow Lord's black magic, was hunting its next victim. The FireIce fed on fear and potent emotions, and it craved all life force. Its tar-like ooze spread under the ground and burst out to devour its prey with scalding acid. Anvyartach unleashed it in Finnis Fews, curious to know how effective a weapon it might be. So far its rapacious appetite hadn't disappointed him.

This menace had worked its way into Oelsa's dreams and set Fial's nerves on edge. Although Fial had no way of knowing about the FireIce, his senses jangled as it oozed closer.

Fial paused under a tree and whispered to the shadowy form sitting on the limb over his head. "Biab, I know you're up there."

She dropped like a rock onto his shoulder. "How did you see me?"

"More to the point, why are you here at all?"

"You're not the only one who can creep through the woods in the dark."

"That seems quite clear, but why are you following me this time?" Fial's words carried a hint of reprimand. Biab had been ordered many times to stay with the rookery birds at night and not to wander off on her own. Each time she'd acted as though she understood, yet here she was, sitting on his shoulder, a companion he hadn't invited.

Biab shook her feathers and pinched his ear.

Rubbing the spot, Fial said, "You're here now. Ride with me if you like. Or circle overhead and try to keep up. It's your choice."

He sprinted away, his sudden movement almost knocking Biab off his shoulder. She gripped his cloak with her strong claws. "You'd like me to fall, wouldn't you, Magician?"

"Have you sensed anything not belonging here, Biab?"

"No." The exertion of holding on to his cloak was tiring. "But I'm just as good at finding straws in the dark as you are."

"You could be right." Fial worked his way past a clump of alder. "Let's hope we don't find anything more than we can handle."

As Fial circled the ravens' night camp, he sensed fear among the trees and animals. But an hour later, they had found no evidence of an enemy near their encampment.

When Biab's legs cramped from holding onto Fial's shoulder, he paused long enough to gently scoop her into the crook of his arm. She tried to keep her eyes open, but the long day of searching for the girl's father had worn her out. Soon her head was bobbing. Tenderly Fial tucked her under his cloak.

5

"WHAT A NUISANCE! This wretched gorse is everywhere, and my cape is catching on every barb and thorn," G. W. L'Aege, the old wizardess, grumbled as she walked. Wisps of white hair slipped from the knot at the back of her head and framed her wrinkled face. When she stopped to work the cape's richly embroidered corner from a stubborn thorn, a furry, marmalade head poked out of the pack on her back.

"Can't see we've traveled very far," Samson remarked as he assessed the grasslands through which G.W. was walking. His yawn was wide and exaggerated. So bored, it hinted.

G.W. swatted over her head, hoping to catch the impudent feline on the ears. Instead she knocked off her wooly, green hat. "Frizzle frumpers frackenstad."

The orange cat purred and licked a white-tipped paw as he rested against her shoulder. When he spied a movement in the long grass, Samson launched himself from G.W.'s shoulder. After a brief scuffle, he stood with a fat vole clutched between his teeth.

"Drop it, Samson," G.W. scolded. "We haven't time for refresh-

ments, or for frightening the wits out of all the creatures who call this their home."

With a growl, Samson retracted his claws, opened his mouth, and waited for the terrified creature to make a dash for freedom.

G.W. coaxed the little vole. "Go on. He won't bite, will you, Samson?"

"Get along, now. I was just playing. That's a good little fellow." Samson's smile revealed his sharp canines. The frightened vole bolted into the thick grass.

Nodding her approval, G.W. picked up the heavy cat and held him. "You're a good boy at heart." She rubbed him under his chin while Samson butted his head into her hand.

Samson climbed to her shoulder and crawled into the pack. He pawed the wool blanket into a nest before settling down. G.W.'s thoughts focused on the purpose of this unexpected journey.

Disturbing dreams two nights ago had propelled them onto the road across Idelisia. If the images are true, she thought, the danger may have already reached the woodcutter and his daughter. This thought pushed G.W. to pick up her pace.

As she walked, G.W. recalled the stories her great grandmother had told about the first war that nearly destroyed Idelisia. The First Creators had vanquished the rebellious Anvyartach but only after a terrible struggle. The stories said he was gone forever, but G.W.'s and Samson's dreams contradicted the old stories.

When an image of Anvyartach, the Shadow Lord, flashed through her mind, G.W. shivered and thought, *If he does return, this time he'll be angrier . . . and much stronger.*

G.W. cut a *V* through the thick grasses and returned to the dream images. A golden Key hovered before her face, so bright she could barely see. When she covered her eyes, the Key pressed against her eyelids. When she peeked through her fingers, the Key was gone, re-

placed by the image of a girl sitting with her back against a tree. A gentle smile played across the girl's lips. From inside the girl, a golden light glowed and G.W. realized, *She is the Key in the First Creators' Prophecy.*

The voice in the dream made G.W. shiver again. She thought, *If the Shadow Lord discovers the girl has the Key, he won't stop until he's wrested it from her. His revenge will be to destroy Idelisia, using the Key.*

The dream's message was clear. *Samson and I must find the girl before he does, and guide her to the awakening of the Key's power. We must find the Heart of the Woods before it's too late.*

Anvyartach sat next to the long, wooden table in his library. Parchment scrolls with curled edges were scattered across it. His slaves had searched every corner of his stronghold and uncovered hundreds of these ancient scrolls hidden everywhere. Many were written in the language and script of the First Creators.

"Here it is!" Anvyartach tensed. Without full recovery, his arm and hand were as likely to crush the fragile manuscript or toss it in the fire as to raise it to his eyes.

Anvyartach pressed the parchment against the table and set a heavy silver candlestick on top to keep it from curling. He scanned the scroll, slowly absorbing its content. "Here's the second mention of a Key, but what is it?" His arm jerked, nearly knocking over the lighted candlestick.

Willing his body to relax, Anvyartach reread the words that had caused him to send Mangred into Finnis Fews. "Not only do they think they've created an invincible weapon to destroy me a second time, but they've imbued it with much more. 'The Key will reveal a great treasure . . .'" He rubbed his eyes before completing the sentence. "'. . . and absolute power!'"

Shaking with avarice, Anvyartach clutched the fragile parchment scroll in his bony hand. "The greatest treasure ever known, and it will soon be mine, all mine! When I hold this golden Key, inlaid with diamonds and rubies and pearls, I'll need both hands it will be so heavy." Wetting his lips, Anvyartach continued to read. When he found a new passage, he smiled. "'One family has been chosen to carry this burden. They alone must bear the secret of the Key.'" He blinked sweat from his eyes. "'The Woodcutter's Clan is so named.'"

Gleefully, Anvyartach leapt to his feet. "The woodcutter! Mangred has captured him and is bringing him here!"

6

A BLURRED IMAGE BURNED through Oelsa's dream. "Father?"

Oelsa gasped and rose onto her elbows. She scanned her surroundings. Cold ashes lay in the fire pit. A faint rustling on her left warned her to duck down and pretend to be asleep. Through her eyelashes she watched Fial slip from the shadows. He smiled as he checked the sleeping ravens. Satisfied all was well, he sat next to the log where Oelsa had last seen him.

Oelsa remained motionless, but doubts niggled at her thoughts. *Why did Fial tell me nothing was wrong, but then go into the woods? Why did Biab follow him? She doesn't even like him, does she?*

The ambiguous scene, the uncertainty of her situation, the violent abduction of her father only days ago—all of Oelsa's fears crushed her spirits. She couldn't stay still another instant. Trying to stay calm, Oelsa hesitated, but more memories crowded into her mind. Why couldn't she wake up and be with her father in their cottage eating breakfast together? It was all she wanted.

Fial shifted positions. Oelsa thought, *Fial's hiding something. He hasn't been completely honest with me.* The forest rustled around them.

Oelsa's eyes darted everywhere as she searched the darkness. Fear and uncertainty pushed Oelsa to her knees. She gripped her pack in her right hand, ordered herself to stand, and fled into the forest night.

At that same moment, exactly where Oelsa had been sleeping, the FireIce erupted. Its corrosive ooze blackened the grass and viciously burned the tree's thick roots. A putrid stench filled the campsite.

Choking, Fial leapt up and shouted a warning. The startled ravens lifted from the trees, circled high overhead, and disappeared. Fial moved cautiously toward the invader, gathering the strongest spell he knew to him.

As the murderous fumes thickened the air, Fial hurled the magic spell at the ooze, but it defied him. The FireIce hissed and screamed, filling Fial's nostrils with venomous poison. Fial reached into the deepest recesses of his mind and unloosed all the buried threads of his power. He opened himself to the Old Magic, letting it fill him until he could contain no more. Arcane magic poured into his mind. The light grew until he held an incandescent, blinding ball between the palms of his hands. His muscles ached with the burden of this great sphere, and still the power grew. When the magical force seemed it would consume him, Fial closed his eyes, lifted his chin, and gave a great shout. The phosphorescent mass exploded in the center of the black ooze.

The FireIce screamed and evaporated in a flash.

When Fial at last lowered his arms, the raven troop surrounded him. Their carks and trills and praise poured around him while Fial trembled from every part of his body. Biab gently touched him with her wing and guided him to sit down. Drained by the powerful magic, he stared at the scorched place where the girl had been sleeping.

"Did the girl attack you, Fial?"

"Where is she?" he muttered as he transformed back into raven form.

Shaking his head, Fial called for quiet. "That was the strongest foe I've ever faced. We have to leave this place. Now. Bring the girl!"

Only a reeking hole remained where Oelsa had been sleeping. No one had seen her disappear seconds before the attack. Fial hopped to the edge, sensing only the ooze and the tingling aftermath of its brutal attack.

A quick search turned up a small blue button. Fial said, "She must have lost this when she . . . when she . . ."

Biab finished the sentence. "When she was taken?"

"Yes, when she was taken. What else could have happened?"

"Maybe she ran off. Did she promise to stay with our troop?"

Fial's neck feathers bristled. "No, she made no promises. What of it?"

"Maybe she began to doubt a bunch of birds could help her find her father. We haven't had much luck so far," Biab responded. "She loves him. He's the only person she's ever known."

This possibility hadn't occurred to Fial. "A reasonable explanation." He nodded. "That vicious ooze seemed drawn to the spot where Oelsa was sleeping, but that's crazy. Isn't it?"

No one answered.

"My recent visions," Fial said, "have suggested a malevolent force is growing underground, but I've had no hint that Oelsa is the target." His flattened feathers showed his worry. Lowering his voice, he added, "I was lucky this time, lucky to destroy it. Next time, I may not be so lucky."

Surprised, Biab stared at Fial. His despair touched her. She said, "I agree we need to move from here. If the girl has run away, there's no time to spare."

Fial shook off the lingering horror of the battle. "The girl can't have gone far. The sooner we leave this place, the sooner we'll find her."

When he rose into the air, the raven troop lifted in a blur of wings and, like a dark arrow, shot over the deep forest and out of sight.

7

OELSA MADE HER WAY through the forest night. She slipped her hand into her pocket and ran her fingers over the worn fabric she'd torn from his shirt. "I will find you."

The sounds of struggle she heard as she darted into the woods frightened her. *Maybe Fial is angry and aimed some kind of magic at my back.* She pushed harder to distance herself from the raven encampment.

"Don't look back, just keep moving," she repeated as she pushed through the tangled undergrowth and towering trees.

Scant light filtered to the forest floor when dawn edged over the trees. Exhausted, Oelsa slipped down against the trunk of a gnarled tree. Too tired to move, she grasped her knees and let the hopelessness she'd kept at bay wash over her. "I can't do this," she wept and closed her eyes against the storm of fear building in her chest. The weight of her task bore into her.

"Speak to me, Father. I heard you before I ran." Although the voice she heard wasn't exactly like her father's, who else could it have been?

A thin ray of sunlight filtered through the trees' canopy and touched Oelsa's forehead. Smiling, Oelsa said, "Thank you. I know you'll help me find you." She stood, brushed off the leaves, and noticed a small patch of bushes covered in late season berries.

She crammed the delicious red berries into her mouth as fast as she could pick them. She licked her fingers for every drop of sweetness. Refreshed, she set off to find water. A small pool of clear water trickled over a rock ledge, and she scooped a handful into her mouth.

"That's what I needed." She rested next to the pool. In moments, her shoulders drooped and eyes closed. Her last thought was, *I could stay here forever.*

Oelsa's dream came from a story Dahvi told her a long time ago. The fabled Tower of Kedric, he said, had risen from a vast lake at the eastern edge of Finnis Fews, and it had been at the heart of every story Dahvi told about the early days of Idelisia.

In the dream, Oelsa watched as twenty-five-foot waves crashed against the resilient Tower for days. These were fiercer than any waves ever seen in Idelisia, each crash like a giant's mouth trying to devour the tower's foundation. Day after day, Anvyartach hurled the waves at the Tower. He grew angrier and angrier as it continued to resist. The Tower was protecting the First Creators who had taken refuge inside and were valiantly struggling to halt his destruction of Idelisia.

Storms battered the Tower until the First Creators of Idelisia, sheathed in indestructible cloaks of power, rose up and struck the heart of Anvyartach's stronghold. The first touch of their amassed magic cracked the Shadow Lord's grip on the world. Giant chunks of rock cracked from his fortress, and his attempt to use the forces of nature against Idelisia was broken.

The First Creators continued their attacks until they crushed the Shadow Lord's power and took him captive. Without the Tower's indefatigable resistance, the First Creators would not have had time to combine their powers. Without the Tower's protection, they would not have survived Anvyartach's plan to make Idelisia his own private place of torment.

In the dream, Oelsa heard her father speak the same words he had always used to end his stories: "When the villainous Shadow Lord was finally overpowered and cast into oblivion, the Tower glowed one last time with a golden light, straightened to its full height, and sank under the waves, never to be seen again."

His voice was wistful as he added, "One day, Oelsa, we'll journey east to find the truth about the fabled tower. When the time comes, the Tower will answer all our questions."

Waking from her dream, Oelsa thought, *What if the story of the Tower isn't just a story? Could it still exist?* She stared into the forest and whispered the question closest to her heart. "Could the Tower help me find you, Father?"

The shelves in the library looked as though a storm had blown over them. Books were strewn over the floor where Anvyartach had thrown them in his frenzied search. He slumped in a tall chair next to the heavy wooden table where a dozen candles burned in the candelabrum.

"None have what I want," he whined as he absently reached for a small volume fastened with a thin, leather cord. He pulled on the cord and opened the brittle pages. He stared at the words written in script so elaborate they defied reading.

"These are no ordinary words," he said. "They're completely foreign."

In a roaring fit of temper, Anvyartach threw the fragile book across the room and kicked through the jumble of books scattered on the floor. "They've changed the words. My enemies changed the words to a code I'll never be able to read!"

In his rage he had failed to notice a significant detail at the bottom of the book's front page. Tiny, nearly invisible letters spelled the author's name—Nuala Ni L'Aege, the many-greats grandmother of G. W. L'Aege and a woman Anvyartach had once known extremely well.

8

ARMS SWINGING AT HER SIDES, Oelsa followed the meandering stream, determined to reach the eastern edge of the great forest, find the Tower, and maybe even save her father before the day ended. Birds twittered overhead and the sun glinted off the singing water.

Hours later, Oelsa no longer could see the stream as she staggered around another thorny bush. When she came up against yet another enormous cedar, she shouted, "Move!" She shoved on its trunk, but the tree didn't budge. She kicked it and limped on through the dense forest. Vines hung from tree limbs and tangled in her hair. Spiders ran over her head and arms as she swept through sticky cobwebs.

"I said I would find you, Father, and I will," Oelsa told herself, but with every step she felt less certain, and when she noticed the same bush with white flowers she'd seen an hour earlier, she realized she was going in circles.

She searched the ground for pebbles to mark her trail but found only broken twigs and dried pine needles. She grabbed a handful and began dropping them behind her. But when she reached down for more and looked back the way she had come, she couldn't tell where she'd just walked.

"I give up." She leaned against a tall pine and rubbed her nose with the back of her hand. Wind ruffled the trees' top branches. Nocturnal animals scrambled through the woods pursuing their nightly business. Darkness settled into the woods long before night fell and with it the number of rustling sounds increased while tiny eyes blinked from the shadows.

A sound startled her.

"What's that? Is someone there? I've got a stick, a big one." She crouched and searched around her, hoping to see a branch large enough to ward off an attacker. When no new sound came, Oelsa gradually relaxed. "Just my imagination." Her fingers trembled when she touched the ties on her cloak. "I'll be fine," she whispered, "just fine." Huddled against the tree, Oelsa decided to find a safe place for the night.

She pushed away from the tree trunk and tripped. Too tired to rise, Oelsa made herself crawl through the undergrowth. "A little cave or a dry spot under some low-hanging branches. That's all I need." Unexpectedly, her hand touched something cold and squishy. It moved. She screamed, leapt to her feet, and ran blindly, colliding with the unyielding trunk of an enormous fir. She staggered and fell hard.

Miles away FireIce, from its underground hiding spot, caught a faint whiff of fear, but it was so far away. Other sources of dread were much closer and so much easier to devour. It would pursue the fear some other time.

Blurred images floated through her mind. Oelsa gasped at the richness of details: an open field in which thousands of beings—humans, animals, birds, flowers, trees, and plants of every kind—surrounded her. Radiant light bathed Idelisia's multitude of inhabitants. Oelsa's spirit lifted from her body, looked down at her still form, and drifted toward the center of the gathering.

As she glided over this world, Oelsa noticed an ornate golden Key the size of her palm floating before her eyes. Ancient symbols were etched along its sides and twined over every surface of the Key.

The Key sparkled and danced before her, but each time she reached for it, it winked out of sight. The moment she lowered her hands, however, the Key reappeared and enticed her to reach again. The more she gazed at the glorious Key, the more Oelsa longed to touch it.

Absorbed by the captivating vision of the illusive Key, Oelsa drifted in the glow of its beauty, happy to be in its presence.

In time, Oelsa's spirit reached a towering peak and the grandeur of Idelisia spread before her. Perfect harmonies from all of Idelisia's inhabitants rose in celestial strands of song that filled her with the pure majesty of Idelisia until she radiated with peace.

So perfect was this sensation, she failed to notice when clouds like purple bruises piled on top of each other. A stunning flash scorched her eyelids. The tranquil world in which she floated dissolved, and Oelsa plummeted toward an angry, rock-strewn sea with knife sharp stones rising from the water.

Thrusting out her hands to break her fall, she was certain she would be dashed to pieces. She slammed against the hard surfaces and bounced from rock to rock. When she finally stopped, she expected her body to be torn and broken against the stones. Miraculously, she remained intact, but instead of landing on ground, she balanced precariously on the edge of a crumbling structure whose bricks and mortar were collapsing into a calamitous waterfall. Hopelessness flooded her. Her earlier peace was crushed by the weight of the destruction around her. She begged, "No more. Let me be!"

Voices keened, "The Key! Use the Key before he binds us forever to eternal torment and suffering."

A thin gold chain was fastened around her neck. Oelsa laid her finger on it and the ornate Key materialized in her fingers. She could feel its weight and warmth against her skin. The brief moment of hope was dashed as the chain broke, and the Key flew out into the vast universe.

"There it is!" A skeletal finger pointed skyward, and Oelsa turned in time to see the golden Key rotating end over end, growing smaller and dimmer as it hurtled into the darkness. Oelsa willed herself to fly upward, but before she could reach the delicate Key, a voice cried, "Over there! Near the blackened planet shrouded in shadows! It's almost there!"

The tumbling Key spun away into the crowded cosmos, where planets and stars and comets whirled, and collided in brilliant flashes. As the Key spun away, Oelsa reached for it. Instead she spiraled in the opposite direction, into the absolute cold of outer space.

A new horror waited for her. Its voice, like claws dragged over stone, stabbed her ears. A hideous face, contorted with rage, loomed over Oelsa. Its red eyes blazed with madness. Threats poured into her head. "Idelisia is mine. You cannot hide the Key forever. Tell me where it is hidden and your torment will end."

"I don't know where it went!"

The specter responded by surrounding her with roiling clouds, at the center of which her father writhed in pain. The hideous presence hissed, "Bring me the Key or his torment will never end."

Oelsa jerked awake shaking so hard she had to clamp her arms around her sides. The nightmare played over again and again in her mind, and she sobbed. Alone in the immense forest, plagued by horrific visions, terror choked her. Never had she felt such utter abandonment.

A faint sensation nudged her heart. She reached under her cloak and grasped the yellow stone. Instantly her racing pulse slowed and comfort spread through her. Oelsa's trembling subsided as the yellow stone restored her courage. Fial's gift had more to it than translating bird sounds.

Oelsa shivered again as she remembered the specter's voice. "Such a coldhearted ghoul. What could that beautiful Key have to do with him—or me?"

9

RAIN FELL WITH INCREASING FORCE as G.W. hurried through
the tall grasses. "Stay put, Orange Fluff. Your whiskers will get soaked
and then what will you do?" The old wizardess hurried toward the
protection of the looming trees.

Ignoring G.W.'s directions, Samson emerged from the backpack,
paused, and leapt to the ground. "See you when you get there!" he
called as he disappeared from view.

G.W. pushed harder to reach the edge of the great forest. "Just
like a cat."

"Why must everything be so hard?" Each time Anvyartach tried to call
up the vision of Mangred and his crew of ruffians, he could only catch
glimpses through the murky glass, and each glimpse showed them either bogged down in a swampy area or hindered by overgrown trees.

"I should have given him something to blast those miserable
trees to smithereens!" As he held the glass orb closer to his face,
Anvyartach's right eye rolled to the side and tried to disappear to the
back of his head.

Anvyartach shook his head violently.

When he again looked into the orb, Mangred had disappeared as well as the log and the soldiers carrying it. "Now what?" he cried. "This stupid orb is worthless." Before he could throw it across the room, his arm gave way, and the orb rolled into his lap. "Aiee! Why me?" Slumped on the throne, Anvyartach's shoulders sagged and his head bent onto his chest. Disconsolate, he repeated a thought that had bothered him for several days. "Someone besides this woodcutter is out there. I can sense another presence, but I can't uncover where, or who."

Unable to sit still, the Shadow Lord lurched down the marble steps, headed for the library, and grabbed a book from the shelf. Before he read more than the title, he complained, "Useless. Useless scribblings. Why don't they ever tell me something important, like where exactly that blasted Key is located?"

Staring vacantly, Anvyartach thought, *There was one book the last time I was in here, one with the indecipherable words. Where did I put that?*

The floor was littered with discarded books.

"Find the one with the strange words!" Anvyartach ordered a slave, who immediately crawled through the jumble of torn books and pages.

Anvyartach attacked the books on the table, ripping off covers, roughly pawing through their pages. *More dreary dates. All I want to know is what preparations they made to thwart me if, against all odds, I were to return.* He snorted. *Of course, they thought I was gone for good!*

The Shadow Lord threw book after book to the floor. *The Key has to be the answer for my revenge. They can't hide it from me forever. I want it. It's mine!*

The book with the strange words was under Anvyartach's foot, but he was so preoccupied by his thoughts of revenge that he failed to notice it.

10

G.W. HAD BEEN DREAMING of black, amorphous pools with sentient thoughts of devouring her and every living thing around her. "What a night," she said. "Glad to wake up from such wretched dreams." She pushed the blanket into her pack and looked at the thick wall of trees. "I'll be happier when we've found the girl and her father."

Without warning, Samson smacked into her, his breath coming in gasps. "Get moving!"

Too startled to object, G.W. grabbed her pack and pushed through the trees. "Where are you, Sam?"

Samson's whiskers and sensitive paws detected a path and G.W. scrambled after him. As her eyes adjusted to the twilight of Finnis Fews, G.W. saw an orange tuft of hair caught on a branch.

"I'm straight ahead. Keep your head down!"

G.W. cracked her forehead on a thick branch. The thick foliage muffled her yelp.

The going was nearly impossible. Samson kept looking over his shoulder and urging G.W. to move faster. When they paused, an evil smell reached them, and Samson cried, "It's racing across the grass-lands. Run!"

G.W. had time to take one quick look and stopped dead in her tracks. The black ooze engulfed everything in its path, obliterating it all in a blistering fire. The forest screamed in terror and pain.

"Move, G.W.!"

But the old wizardess could not abandon the living forest around her. This was an abomination like none she had ever seen and it had to be stopped. She pulled her wand from her cloak and held it in front of her with both hands, closed her eyes, and let the words from spells older than the ancient woods pour from her.

The black ooze paused its devouring of a stand of oaks and sniffed the air. Magic was an alluring smell and beckoned it like no other force had. Mindlessly craving every emotion, the FireIce could not resist the power of this magic. Like an arrow, it leapt forward and landed only a few feet away from G.W. and her wand.

Surprised by the wall of resistance, the FireIce paused. Nothing had stopped it before. Gathering itself into a mighty coil of rage, the FireIce focused solely on the wave of light standing before it.

It sprang with no warning. Without the wand's strength, G.W. would have been devoured. Samson raced back to his friend, un-leashed his chilling battle cry, and sent wave after wave of magic into the foul force before them.

Yowling like a fiend, Samson leapt toward the FireIce and would have been incinerated if G.W. hadn't grabbed his tail and swung him out of range at the last moment.

She whirled back toward the horror and called on the powers of the Grandmothers, the same ancient power that had, once upon a time, quelled the madman of the First Creators. Wrapped in centuries of L'Aege women's might, G.W. advanced toward the FireIce. With each step she hurled rings of the ancient magic into its heart.

Screaming and writhing upward again and again, the FireIce

fought back, but it could not break the power sent from the enraged wizardess.

"Surrender!" G.W. commanded.

The FireIce sank below the ground and fled.

G.W. bowed her head. "What has he done?" She shuddered at the swath of charred and stinking holes left from this vicious attack. If G.W. had any doubts before that the Shadow Lord had returned to Idelisia intent on destroying every particle of the world she loved, she didn't now.

The light touch on her arm made G.W. scream. "No more!" She held her wand in a protective stance. Her hands trembled so hard she almost dropped it.

"There now. It's just me." Samson purred and rubbed his head against her legs. "You almost tore my tail off just now. Where did you get such a hefty swing?" His presence calmed G.W.

"I was worried you might have lost your touch, but you certainly showed me." He licked his tail and winced.

"Oh, Samson, I was so terrified you'd be destroyed by that wicked, wicked thing." She pulled him onto her lap. "I couldn't bear to lose you, dear one."

Samson allowed himself to be hugged for a few moments, then wriggled out of his friend's arms. "Let's find some water. I'm parched."

G.W. staggered into the trees, listening for the sounds of the cat's passage. The quieting of birds' calls guided her forward until she found him sitting next to a lovely stream. "Bless you, Samson."

Both woman and cat stuck their faces into the cold water. When they drank their fill, they sat back on the grassy bank.

"What just happened?" G.W. asked. "I have never seen anything like that . . . that . . ." She couldn't finish the sentence as the horror washed over her again.

"I don't think there is a word for that," Samson said. "I barely had time to warn you, it moved so quickly."

As he told G.W. of setting off for his morning meal, he watched her face to see how she was recovering from her extraordinary expenditure of magical energy. Grandmothers or not, G.W. had called upon old and mysterious powers. The cost to her would be heavy, and he worried how quickly she would recover.

"The truth is I was terrified, but just as it slithered toward me, I tripped on a burrow entrance and fell down a woodchuck's hole. Had it not been for that, I'd have been incinerated right there and then."

"How did you manage to get back to me so quickly?" G.W. asked.

"Luck again. The woodchuck had burrowed deep enough to escape. When he ran for his back door, I followed. When we emerged close to our campsite, I'm not sure if I ran or flew to you."

"This is worse than I imagined, Samson. He has returned just as my great grandmother warned. He won't stop until he's taken his revenge, and we've had a small taste of what he's capable of."

Samson shivered in spite of his strong desire not to. He wanted G.W. to believe he was unscathed by this attack and could, and would, protect her no matter what. "We need to move," he said. "I don't know where that thing went, but I bet it isn't done with us."

"You're right. The girl is in greater danger than I dreamed."

G.W. pulled the map from the inside pocket of her cloak, laid it on the ground, and smoothed out the edges. Using her wand for light, she placed her finger on the map and traced along one of the streams. She felt a faint tingle in her fingertip. "This way, Sam."

Samson leapt to her shoulder and worked his way into the backpack. "You are a queen of women, Grammy Wizard L'Aege. Lead on."

The large raven sitting in a nearby pine lifted into the air and flew after them.

11

SUNRISE LIT THE WOODS with a lilac hue, but a whiff of the destroyed ooze drifted over the ravens' campsite, spoiling the beauty of the morning. When the scouting parties returned to the clearing where Fial paced around the cold campfire, Brand'oo, the leader of the search, *kek-kek-kek'd*.

Fial glanced up. "Well?"

Brand'oo shook his head.

Fial resumed pacing. *One more mystery to solve*, he thought. No matter how many times he went over the facts, Fial couldn't understand what actually happened to Oelsa, or what that twelve-year-old must have been thinking to make her run away.

At bedtime, she seemed tired, but she hadn't given any indication she wanted to escape. Did she know the ooze was about to strike? How long before its strike did she disappear? She did disappear before it struck, didn't she? That was too gruesome a thought to dwell on.

He continued to pace, considering Biab's alternate scenario that the girl ran away. This bothered him more than he wanted to admit.

Maybe the girl didn't trust him. Given the unusual way they met, she'd have little reason to trust him, a complete stranger. But she had willingly joined him.

Fial stopped near Biab's tree. She was humming a tune that calmed restless raven fledglings. "This isn't lullaby time, Biab! We've got a girl to find."

Calling to the troop, Fial announced, "The assembly is convened!"

Neck feathers ruffled and ear feathers lifted in imperious displays. The flock settled in a large circle around their leader. Biab remained perched on a low branch, her eyes hooded. "What report do you have for the morning's search?" Fial called to Brand'oo.

Brand'oo related the details, at the end of which he hung his head and stepped back. Failure did not sit well with Fial's second-in-command.

"Not good enough," Fial said. "Our lives depend on her, whether you believe this or not."

Shifting from foot to foot, the raven leader weighed the consequences of sharing all he knew with them. Too little information and they'd remain unconvinced of the girl's importance. Too much and they might be too frightened to continue the search.

Finally, he said, "There's something I haven't told you."

The ravens' clacking beaks rose to a great din.

"An evil force is building in the north and will soon threaten our homes. The girl is our only defense."

Voices from the troop trilled. "That girl? Our defense? You must be kidding!"

"You doubt my words? If we allow her to disappear into the big woods, what should we do next? Go about our usual business until that ooze returns?" Fial glared at his troop.

Feathers rustled and bills snapped uneasily. The ooze residue smoldered under the tree and was a grim reminder of the near destruction from which Fial had saved them.

Unwilling to concede to Fial, Biab said, "The scouts have, thus far, failed to find her. Whether she's some great savior or not—and I have my doubts that a girl this young could be anything more than a nuisance . . ." Biab halted when she glanced at Fial. His displeasure smoldered as he lifted his eye feathers, but many in the group *tok-tok-tokked* in agreement.

Feeling the weight of responsibility for the whole clan—both those in agreement with her and those who would remain loyal to Fial no matter what—Biab chose her next words more carefully than usual. "We all agree that finding her will be difficult." No one disagreed. "We need a fresh approach."

Fial stared into Biab's eyes, his dark mood pinning her in place. When he replied, his words surprised them all. "Biab is correct."

While the ravens lifted their wings and puffed out their ears and necks, Fial continued, "Tell us your plan, Biab. We're running out of time."

Biab's plan included sending more squads to search below the tree canopy, but after searching for several hours, the ravens returned without any new information.

Fial asked Biab, "How far can a girl move in one night?"

When Biab didn't respond, Fial looked up to the beech trees where the flock had settled. They alternated between preening and stretching and pecking at twigs for insects. They were exhausted.

Fial flew to the top of the tallest tree, commanding the best view of the vast forest. What he saw didn't please him—an endless, impenetrable carpet of green with splashes of reds and golds. Their search seemed hopeless.

Biab chose that moment to practice her more interesting calls. In their clan, she was the recognized expert of expressions. She used her voice and the rearranging of her feathers, as well as various postures, to display a wide range of feelings.

Lifting her head, she sidestepped along the branch in an unusual manner.

Curious, or maybe playful, Fial thought as he watched her.

Next, she violently hammered on her branch and tore off twigs, tossing them and a nearby pinecone to the ground while voicing deep, long, rasping caws. Anger.

She cackled as though a joke known only to her had tickled her, but Fial knew she was aware he was watching.

With dramatic shifts in her posture, Biab ran through her repertoire of *rap-rap-raps*, squeaks followed by low growls and yells. When she reached a particularly loud and long undulating knocking, Fial had enough.

"Stop that racket!"

Biab rose into the air, tumbling like a showy acrobat, and dropped a concealed acorn on Fial's head.

Wincing, Fial bowed to Biab, acknowledging she had the last word. When she set down beside him, she expected a compliment.

"What's your next big idea for finding her?"

Before she could respond, Fial leapt into the air and performed a series of barrel rolls, much to the flock's delight.

12

A DEEP RESTLESSNESS ATE AT ANVYARTACH. "Nothing is going right. Nothing!" His mouth worked to form the words before his tongue and lips quivered uncontrollably. "Bah!" he said as he lurched across the floor toward the book room.

Before he reached the heavy door, however, Anvyartach stopped. "Who said that?" He glared into the shadows. No one stepped forward, but he was certain he heard a voice warning someone to stay away. "From what?" he shouted. "Stay away from what?"

Silence echoed through the hall.

"Aarrgh!" he growled, reaching for the iron-studded, oak door. Touching it, he froze. A vision filled his mind.

In the midst of a ferocious battle of unspeakable carnage, two combatants grappled, locked in a deadly fight. One was a woman warrior wielding a golden sword, and the other, he realized with a start, was him. In the bloody clash, they gripped each other in vise-like holds, staggered, and plunged headlong into icy water.

As they sank deeper and deeper, they clutched at each other's throats, falling farther into the cold darkness. When Anvyartach thought his lungs would burst, and his opponent would surely best him, a strange sensation pooled around his heart. Dark magic, ripening with time and rage as he drew his scattered body together, erupted with an invincible force. It was power like none Anvyartach had ever felt.

A fierce jubilation coursed through the Shadow Lord as he and his opponent shot out of the water. His hands were still wrapped around her neck.

Anvyartach blinked and the vision faded. "Oh, the power! More than I had the first time." His body shook so hard he had to sit down and brace his back against the door. "Such power. My power." He hugged his knees and shouted until his voice cracked. "I WILL WIN!"

13

OELSA'S BODY ACHED. Her thoughts were filled with frightening images from her vision. She looked around. The fallen part of the ancient fir against which she'd knocked her head stretched into the dark forest and out of sight. "How could I not see you last night," she said as she rubbed the knot on her forehead. "You're enormous."

Resting her hand on the fallen tree trunk, Oelsa wondered which way was east. When a sliver of light broke through the tree canopy, she was sure her plan to reach the Tower was still valid. "If that's east, perhaps today is the day I'll find the Tower and ask how to find Father."

As she stepped away from the fallen fir tree, she touched the yellow stone. "Do you think this is east?" she asked as cheerily as she could. A tickling sensation crossed her palm. "Off I go, then. Wish me luck."

A deep rumbling, like the clearing of a throat, stopped Oelsa in her tracks. "You're off quite early, child. You haven't even told us your name." The ancient fir spoke with a gentle authority.

Startled to hear any voice in the middle of Finnis Fews, but especially that of a tree, Oelsa searched for a polite answer. "Oh, don't worry about me. I'm only a child, no one you'd be interested in." She inched toward the edge of the clearing, hoping the fir wouldn't notice.

"Well, Onlyachild, my name is Tallach, Protector of the Ancients. Powerful images filled your mind last night, did they not?"

How could the tree know? "Actually, my name isn't 'Onlyachild.'" She hoped to distract this strange tree long enough to escape.

"Forgive me, but that is what you said, is it not? 'I am Onlyachild'?" Oelsa laughed. "Yes, you're right. That's exactly what I said."

Tallach's branches fluttered back and forth. "But perhaps you have a name by which you'd prefer to be called?"

Touched by the thoughtful offer, she said. "I'm Oelsa."

"O-o-o-o-h-h-h-l-l-l-l-suh." Tallach rolled the sounds with plea-sure. "Delightful, O-o-o-h-h-h-l-l-l-suh. Your dreams were eye-opening?"

Oelsa stepped back. "How could you possibly know what I dreamed?"

"You would not be here in the Ring of the Ancients if you were not looking for dreams, nor would you be allowed to leave without something on which to ponder. Were you visited with something important?"

The dream had been so frightening, especially seeing her father's torment, Oelsa realized she had only responded to the extreme emo-tions it stirred. But the fir tree was asking what the images meant. Not sure how much she should reveal to this strange tree, Oelsa said, "They were stunning."

"You had more than one, then. Which one was the most familiar?"

"Seeing my father, but he was in such pain!" She forgot she was going to say as little as possible.

Tallach lowered a branch and touched Oelsa's arm. "Your father carries a special message for you?"

"I think so, but I don't know what. First, I was given a beautiful Key, but it disappeared and I couldn't find it. Then a terrible monster commanded me to give him the Key or else." She choked as she replayed the horrible images. "But why would I have a Key or give it to him?"

"Powerful messages, Onlyachild, I mean O-o-o-o-o-h-l-l-l-l-suh." Compassion filled Tallach's voice. "What shall you do now?"

"I'm going to find the Tower of Kedric and ask it how to find my father. Maybe it can tell me what the dream means, too."

"Beware of these woods, my child. They have been invaded by a malevolent presence that will devour you without a second thought. Seek that which is your heart's purpose if you wish to know the truth." Having given the girl this message, Tallach's attention ebbed and slipped away.

Relieved but still worried, Oelsa grabbed her pack and moved out of the clearing. *So much to think about.* She stepped onto the narrow path leading deeper into the woods.

14

THE SHADOW LORD'S CASTLE was starkly outlined against the ice-covered mountains. Wrapped in a thick, fur cape, Anvyartach revisited the previous day's vision. The sensation of power thrilled him, and he ached to experience it again. It didn't matter who the woman with the golden sword might be. She was clearly no match for him, and that was all he cared about. What a delicious feeling, choking her.

Memories of the First Time played over his mind. None matched this woman. *Who is she? And that exquisite sword! I want that!* The memory thrilled him. *But why are we fighting?* Questions ate at his patience.

"Bring me the glass orb!"

A nearby slave tried to slip away unobserved.

Anvyartach clasped the slave's arm in his claw-like hand. "Bring me my glass orb polished, so I can see my face in it, or you'll wish you never woke up this morning."

Anvyartach let go and the slave reeled backward, tripping over his own feet. In his panic, he knocked against the wooden cradle in which the glass orb rested and sent it rolling down the marble steps. "Aiyee!" he screamed as he grabbed for the ball before it could break.

Snatching the orb from the slave's upraised hands, Anvyartach fumbled with it when his fingers opened instead of closed. Cradling the orb in his arms until he could control his fingers, Anvyartach peered into the cloudy residue and let the words of magic pour out as he rubbed the glass.

> *Ogha, nition, moocro, nante,*
> *Nah-bo, lock shin.*
> *A-gliff, hak tin.*
> *Abeelah, ahber, abeng, freck*
> *Show me the wanderers*
> *Their progress to check.*

The nacreous film that occluded the orb slowly cleared, like smoke drifting up a chimney. Delighted the spell was working, Anvyartach watched as Mangred cracked Velvet across the backs of the men who were doubled over by the weight of the oak log on their shoulders. The orb revealed Mangred's movements, but he couldn't speak to him. He could only watch, frustrated by their slow progress. "Hurry, you fool! The woodcutter won't last forever!"

With a snap of his fingers, the images disappeared. Anvyartach stared at it and rested his chin on his bony fingers. "I will win. The vision promised. The treasure will be mine."

15

THE DREAM CONTINUED TO PLAGUE Oelsa as she pushed through the woods. Such ethereal music, but where could such a place exist? What a magnificent golden Key, but why did it fly away when she reached for it? More frightening was the monster with the scary face. He thought she was keeping something from him, but what could that be?

The steady pulse of the yellow stone, mixed with occasional peeks of sun through the thick tree canopy, convinced Oelsa she was headed toward the Tower of Kedric. However, the grayness of the day, combined with her lingering fear, tested Oelsa's fragile confidence.

She simply couldn't shake the feeling she was being watched. *It's just that dream making me nervous*, she told herself. But every few steps, she glanced over her shoulder.

"I am on the right path," she told the nearest bush. "I will find the Tower and the villains who took my father. You'll see. With every step, I'm getting closer to the Tower and the answers I need."

A strong hand gripped her ankle and yanked her to the ground.

"Hey!" she shouted, but a calloused hand clamped over her mouth and held her in place. A rough shirt brushed against her face. She felt hot breath against her cheek.

"Shut up and don't move." The voice was low and harsh.

Oelsa didn't think. She bit the hand hard and bolted to her feet.

Before she could take more than two steps, she was seized by the waist and shoved to the ground.

"You're not going anywhere, Biter."

She hit the ground hard enough to make her reconsider another attempt to escape.

"Stay there." This was not a suggestion. "If you move again, or bite, I'll slice off your ear."

He disappeared into the underbrush. The crack of a branch was followed by a loud *clang*. Oelsa gulped when he returned, his large boots an inch from her face. She raised her head to see him. He towered over her, a burly man built like an oak. His legs were like tree trunks, his arms thick as branches. He had a barrel chest, a grizzled beard with sticks and leaves in it, and faded blue eyes.

"Who are you?" Oelsa could barely speak.

He put his finger over his lips, signaling her to stay quiet, and motioned with his head that she should follow him. When she didn't move, he carried her under his arm. Dropping her behind a thick copse, he knelt and placed a strong hand on her back to hold her down. Before she could protest, the ground reverberated with heavy footsteps. Half a dozen massive creatures lumbered along the path carrying clubs the size of tree branches and bulging bags leaking a suspicious fluid. They looked like shaggy bears with human faces. Each step covered yards, and they were around the bend and out of sight in moments.

Oelsa looked at her rough captor, but before she could form a word, a coarse voice shouted, "Someone stole our meat!" Howls split the air and a ferocious fight broke out. Bodies thudded against trees and were walloped and whacked. One voice rose over the others. "Stop yer fighting and find the thief. We'll make him beg for mercy when we do."

Their heavy footsteps faded. The rough hand released Oelsa's back. Oelsa glared at her captor. "What gives you the right . . ."

"Don't make a sound until they're gone." The stranger crouched close to her face, winked, and shouldered his way through the trees. Oelsa wondered what that wink meant, but he soon reappeared and signaled her to join him.

"They're gone," he said. He continued to peer after them. When no further sound could be heard, he said. "A nasty group, those ones. Wouldn't want to end up in their stew pot, would you?" His smile erased his grim appearance.

"The look on your face!" He grinned and soon was laughing so hard he had to hold his sides and lean against a nearby tree.

Oelsa wondered if a crazy person had waylaid her. All the indignity she'd felt evaporated as this new worry took its place. While he laughed helplessly would be a good time to escape, she decided. She glanced to her left, readied herself to run, but before she could move, his right arm shot out and blocked her path.

"Not so quick, girl!" Still roaring with laughter, he gripped her arm. "You're not going anywhere until we've had a little talk."

Oelsa couldn't think of a cutting response as she wriggled furiously against his grip.

"Calm down. I'll let go, if you promise not to run for it."

When Oelsa still tried to pull away, he lifted her off her feet until his face was an inch from hers. "Not until you promise. Agreed?"

She nodded, and he dropped her onto the forest floor. Scowling at this big brute, she remained on her hands and knees. "May I move now?"

"As you please." He stepped back.

Oelsa stood slowly, her hands on her hips. "What makes you think you can grab me and throw me around?" She spit the words at him. "I can see for myself you're some kind of idiot." She balled her fists against her waist and shook with anger.

"At least you've not had your brains smashed out of your head." He laughed again, pleased with himself.

Irritated and humiliated as she was, Oelsa did notice his pale blue eyes were relaxed and his voice had lost all its menace.

"Maybe it would help if you gave me a chance to explain, like who those brutes are."

Oelsa relaxed a fraction. "Fine way you have of asking for my cooperation," she spat back. "First, tell me exactly who you are."

"Fair enough. My name is Ardreas GreatOak. I work in these woods."

"Work? You think throwing people around is work?"

His laugh only annoyed her further.

"Okay, I understand you might be a little upset by my, uh, abrupt handling."

"Oh, you think so?" She wanted to slug him.

"But if you had taken one more step back there, you would have tripped a steel trap that very likely would have torn off your leg. And who knows where the next trap might be? Under the circumstances, I thought you might appreciate the help."

Oelsa's mouth fell open.

"These woods are full of nasty traps set by creatures more savage than me. You would have made a tasty morsel for their kettle."

Oelsa gulped and closed her mouth. "What are they?"

"My people call them WilderOnes, and we've had our share of trouble from them ever since they moved into this part of the forest. I've been trying to discourage them from staying around by tripping their traps. No food, no interest in staying. Unfortunately, I haven't been able to find all their traps in time."

Oelsa's curiosity was growing. "But where do you come from and how do you know so much about these creatures?"

Ardreas waited and, when her shoulders dropped and she calmed ever so slightly, he said, "They've moved down from the far north. Last summer we noticed large tree limbs, often covered in blood, thrown here and there. Animals were disappearing and we didn't know why."

"How could you miss those creatures?" Oelsa interrupted. "They're hard to miss."

"We had no idea we were being invaded until it was too late. Nothing like these savages had ever been in our part of Finnis Fews."

Realizing how narrowly she had escaped the trap set by those nasty creatures, Oelsa's legs quivered. The stranger had saved her life. "Thank you. Won't you tell me more about yourself . . . please?"

A smile spread across Ardreas's face and lit up his eyes. He stretched to his full height. "My people are the GreatOak Clan, and we live in a small hamlet called Adare. We are caretakers of these great woods."

He bowed deeply to Oelsa. "And who might you be?"

At that moment, it struck Oelsa how limited her life had been. She had never heard of a settlement called Adare or people whose lives were spent caring for the great forest. Nor had she imagined any creatures in Finnis Fews so evil they used traps to harm its animals.

She had known nothing of this while living in the Heart of the Woods with her father. That safe, protected life was gone, and she was in a much darker, much more dangerous, world.

Oelsa squared her shoulders, lifted her head, and looked directly into the stranger's eyes. "My name is Oelsa, daughter of Dahvi the Woodcutter. I am certain he's been kidnapped, and I must find him before he's killed."

16

ANVYARTACH HOWLED as his leg kicked out to the side and his arm bounced against the vial for which he'd been reaching. He fumbled with the bouncing vial, caught himself on the side of the worktable, and finally clutched the vial against his chest. "Why must I endure these indignities?"

Fear gnawed at Anvyartach each time he worked in his laboratory. One flinch, one uncontrolled spasm, and disaster could strike— broken vials, lost ingredients, scrambled potions, all up in smoke, or worse. He could move from workbench to shelf, pick up glass vials, and will his fingers to hold on to them, but only with absolute concentration.

"I made the right mixture for Mangred, though, didn't I? This time I'm sure I've found the right spell to speak to Mangred using the orb. Just one more pinch and it will be perfect."

Holding the final ingredient, Anvyartach reviewed his plan to bring the Key to him. "The book said the Woodcutter Clan carries the Key." He paused. Doubt ate at his memory. "Or did it say they know the secret to its hiding place?" Indecision and imprecise memory galled him as he tried to recall the exact words. He had thrown that book onto the floor when he'd finished reading it, along with all the many others, making it almost impossible to find.

"Never mind. Mangred's prisoner knows the answer!" His mind churned with schemes to plunder the woodcutter's secrets. "I want to question him *now*. Why should I wait?"

He clapped his hand to his forehead. "Because I haven't finished this potion that is certain to make speaking through the orb possible!"

Impatience boiled inside Anvyartach, and he almost threw the vial holding this most promising potion against the wall. "Calm yourself. One more look at the instructions for Far Speaking." He ran a bony finger down the book. "Here." He mumbled the words: "'Once the final ingredient is added, you have less than a minute to consume it before it evaporates, or . . .' Yes, yes, yes, I get it! Once I swallow it, the mystery of speaking through the orb will be solved. The woodcutter will give me his secrets, and the Key will be mine!"

Anvyartach wrestled with indecision. He swayed as he added the final ingredient to the vial whose viscous gray liquid had a stomach-churning smell. The last powder sank to the bottom of the vial, and the potion changed to a subtle shade of green. The potion slowly began to swirl by itself.

"I don't recall this happening before."

The swirling concoction held his gaze.

The clock ticked.

His eyes glazed as he intoned the powerful incantation.

Camorra, degerate u discerpic.
Inbetat infelcifet, indagat therblige.
Fluud-ist ichanel.
Agamousta! Agamoustet!
Zendetica!

He raised the vial, took a deep breath, and gulped it down. The liquid burned his mouth and set his teeth on edge. His throat hurt and he felt queasy.

Anvyartach waited, but when nothing further happened, he congratulated himself. "The Key is mine!"

In an instant, his hair stood up straight and smoke poured from every strand. He clutched his throat to scream, but no sound came out. Anvyartach's body arched backward. He fell, twitching convulsively on the floor. The vial flew out of his hand and shattered against the wall. The Shadow Lord's eyes bulged as he silently screamed, *Water!*

"Didn't you hear those brutes threatening to 'take care of' the one who's ruining their traps? They're dangerous, Oelsa. This isn't a joke." Ardreas stared as Oelsa started down the path. The yellow stone had indicated this was the way to the Tower of Kedric.

"I don't care. My father is suffering, and I must find him."

"What makes you think that's the right direction?"

Oelsa shrugged. She kept two fingers on the stone and felt its reassuring thrum. "I just know."

"Well, continue that way if you want, but I can guarantee the next thing you find will not be your father. Those WilderOnes are excellent hunters, and they'll have you in a pot before you can blink."

Oelsa halted. "I can't just stand around and do nothing. Every minute I hesitate, he's wondering why I've abandoned him."

She tried to summon up the image of her father as she'd last seen him, but instead she only saw the horrible images from last night's dream. The terrifying face of the fiend swam before her eyes and his threats loomed over her. "He's running out of time." She choked. Her face was white. Her shoulders shook.

The girl's distress touched Ardreas. "I can lead you through this part of the forest. If you'd like, that is. I've a fair notion of where those beasts and their traps are located. We can avoid any more run-ins at least. What do you say?"

She stared at Ardreas. His lips were moving, but Oelsa's mind was in turmoil. Instead of Ardreas's words, she heard a different voice. Bits and pieces of a conversation drifted in and out of her awareness: "last . . . vial . . . orb . . . it's . . . mine . . ." The words were jumbled, but the voice was familiar.

"Did you hear what I just said?" Ardreas noticed how cloudy Oelsa's eyes had become and stared into her face. "You don't look so good, girl. Sit down here." He took her arm and guided her to the ground. "You look like you've seen a ghost."

Shaking her head, Oelsa was startled to see the large man next to her. His voice came to her as if from the bottom of a pool.

She put her hand to her forehead. "I have the strangest sensation, Ardreas. Like I'm hearing a conversation from miles away."

Ardreas frowned and stared at her.

"What if it's Father trying to send me a message?" She leapt up.

Ardreas restrained her. "Maybe you should tell me more about what's going on, Oelsa. You aren't making a lot of sense."

Although she hadn't intended to, Oelsa blurted out last night's dream. She hesitated briefly when she came to the end. "It was so frightening, Ardreas. And the worst part is I have no idea what it means."

"Strange indeed." Ardreas scratched his head. "But I'm more convinced than ever you need me to go with you, at least until we get past the WilderOnes. Agreed?"

"Thank you, Ardreas." She hesitated a moment. "Maybe I should tell you one more thing." She grasped the yellow stone and held it in her palm.

Ardreas smiled, assuming it was merely a piece of jewelry she wore around her neck.

"This stone is guiding me. I can't explain how it works, but when the raven gave it to me—"

"Raven? You mean a bird? Gave you a present?" Amazement and doubt spread over Ardreas's face.

"I know. It's hard to believe, but I'll explain as we go along." She took Ardreas's large hand in her small one. "Ever hear stories about a big lake on the eastern edge of Finnis Fews and the Tower of Kedric?" She held his hand and tugged him along with her as they set off.

"And if you need water, just tell me. We can stop whenever you wish."

Ardreas frowned. He hadn't said anything about water.

17

ANVYARTACH HAD NO IDEA how long he lay on the cold floor. When he opened his eyes, his body was chilled. If he hadn't been wearing the fur cloak, he might have frozen. His joints were stiff, his head throbbed, and his face burned.

The Shadow Lord opened his mouth to call for help. His mouth moved but no sound came out.

Grabbing his neck with both hands, Anvyartach's eyes widened. *What have I done?* He huddled on the floor, quivering. *This isn't what it seems. It's only a temporary setback. Nothing permanent.*

He rolled to his left side and braced himself on his elbow. When nothing gave way, he sat upright.

I can do this. He mouthed the words, but no sound came from his lips.

After several more failed attempts to speak, Anvyartach got on his knees and reached for the edge of the table where he'd mixed the potion. What had gone wrong? He'd followed the steps exactly. Maybe he skipped a *few* parts, but this, this, this . . . His throat was raw. He couldn't make a sound.

He tried sighing. Nothing.

A fierce growl built inside him, but he couldn't release it. He screwed his eyes tight, curled his lips, bared his teeth, and willed himself to roar. Nothing happened. *No, no, no, no! This can't be happening to me!* The Shadow Lord was mute.

He grasped the worktable and pulled himself up. His vision blurred. Odd images jumbled in his mind. He heard a child's voice.

The book on which the potion was written lay where he'd tossed it aside. He picked it up, scanned the instructions, and stopped. He thought, *What have I done? This spell isn't for speaking into an object, like the orb, but into . . .* He skipped to the last words and saw his mistake: "Danger! Do not drink until the swirling has stopped. To do so will damage your voice, perhaps forever."

Anvyartach steadied himself against the side of the table. *Forever?* Panicked, the Shadow Lord hobbled to the door, opened it, and stumbled out. Screaming inside his head, Anvyartach mouthed, "Help me!" again and again until one of the slaves noticed.

Two more slaves grasped Anvyartach's arms to support him. Anger rolled off the Shadow Lord as they guided him to a chair. Gesturing wildly, he managed to convey they should take him to his room. Once there, he collapsed onto his bed and pounded it violently. Humiliation! He couldn't bear such humiliation!

Terrified by their Master's silent rage, the slaves backed out of the room and disappeared. Exhausted, Anvyartach lay in a daze until more unusual images filled his head. This time he saw a girl and heard her words about a missing person. Did she say her father was missing? He listened harder as the voice said clearly, "I have to find him before it's too late."

An idea formed in Anvyartach's mind, more useful than any he'd had yet. *This girl was talking about her father being taken. Did she mean the woodcutter? Could she be of the Woodcutter Clan as well? If so, she knew where the Key was as well.*

The realization staggered Anvyartach. As this new possibility sank in, he recalled the words before the warning: He could speak into minds. This was why he could hear the strange child's voice.

"I have an idea where those villains are taking your father," Ardreas said as they walked. "You said they were headed north, yes?"

Oelsa, lost in her own thoughts, nodded absently.

Ardreas stopped as they entered a clearing. He picked up a stick, smoothed an area of dirt, and drew a large circle. Pointing to the circle, he said, "This is where we are in Finnis Fews." He drew a line to another point in the circle. "Given the length of time you've been gone, I'd guess your home is about here." He drew an X.

"My home in Adare is about here." He put another X on the circle. "This is where I calculate we met." He put a third X on the circle closer to Adare than to her home in the Heart of the Woods.

"If the ones who took your father are heading north from your home," he said, drawing a line to the top of the circle, "I suspect our paths might intersect somewhere around here." He drew another line leading north.

"It's hard to know how fast they're moving," he said, "but I do know that part of Finnis Fews is next to impossible to navigate."

"But I thought we were headed east," Oelsa said, "to the Tower. That's what we agreed to do."

"I know," Ardreas said. "That is what we decided when we set out. But now, well, I think we're being followed."

"What?"

"I haven't seen anyone, but something doesn't feel right. It's not WilderOnes. We'd smell them a long way off. But something's different, and it feels wrong."

"What are you saying, Ardreas?"

"What if the Tower is just a story? What if it isn't there? Didn't you say it disappeared? We need another plan, just in case. That's why I think we have a better chance to intercept your father's kidnappers going my way."

Oelsa plopped onto the ground. Her arms fell to her sides. Her eyes were glassy and vacant.

"Oelsa? What's wrong? Can you hear me?" Ardreas waved a hand in front of her face.

"Do you feel sort of odd, Ardreas, like something might be poking your brain with a stick?"

Alarmed, Ardreas stared at her. "Not really. What's happening to you?" He crouched next to Oelsa. She stiffened, eyes blank, face twisted with pain.

"Wake up, girl! Can you hear me?"

Oelsa held her head and moaned. "That voice. I hear that voice, but I can't understand what he's saying."

18

G.W. AND SAMSON PUSHED THROUGH Finnis Fews. The forest was like a tangled maze with no clear path leading anywhere.

"Are we going anywhere, Sam?" G.W.'s voice was tinged with exhaustion. Fighting the black ooze had forced her to go deep into her reserves of energy and magic, and recovering was harder than she wanted to admit.

Samson rested on her shoulder, his back legs propped against the pack's top. "I need to be on the ground where I can sniff out which direction to take." He leapt down and lifted his top lip sideways, making a *flehming* sound.

Turning her map this way and that, G.W. said, "I should have listened better to the tales my great grandmother told about this old forest. She said there was a good reason no one could draw a decent map of this big forest. I'm beginning to understand why."

"Come on, G.W. I think I have a whiff of something we can follow." Without waiting for an answer, Samson disappeared into the underbrush.

Shouldering her way through the trees, G.W. bent down, trying to see which direction the cat had gone. "Where are you, Orange Puff? All I see are thick clumps of cedar and fir."

The orange cat slipped back to G.W. "Too tight, eh? Maybe I can find a better place." He disappeared again. G.W. tripped over the tangled roots of an ancient tree that had fallen so long ago seedlings were sprouting from its side.

"Oof!" She caught herself on the leaning trunk of a dead snag. "Talk to me, Orange Pants, or I'll never find you."

A muffled meow came from a thick patch of prickly diablo plants. "It almost seems this forest doesn't want any visitors." G.W. pushed toward the rustling sounds Samson was making.

The two friends clambered over the thick growth of the old forest. When the canopy opened briefly, sunlight filtered down giving G.W. a chance to rest her straining eyes. Samson's feline ability to see was superior, but he too welcomed the brief, cheery moments that were quickly swallowed as they plunged through more stands of tumbled trees.

The thick air was hard to breathe, although it carried enticing waves of scent to Samson. "Too bad we can't eat these delicious aromas," he called to his companion. Her "hrrumph!" didn't surprise him.

Staggering around another fallen tree, G.W. called a halt. "If I brush into another cobweb ever again, it will be too soon," she groaned. "You don't smell any stench, do you, like that, you know. . ." She meant the black ooze.

"Not since yesterday, although I can't seem to shake the notion it's following us. You too?"

The sensation of being stalked grew in G.W., but she had no intention of telling Samson. He was working hard enough sensing their way through the dismal gloom.

"By the way, Orange Wonder, do you have a plan for finding this Heart of the Woods, or do you think your general good luck will guide you there? Just asking," she teased as she wiped sweat from her face and staggered on.

"Do you hear that?" Samson called from several feet ahead.

G.W. didn't notice anything except more moss-covered logs. When she caught up to him, Samson pointed toward a clearing in the dense forest where a cottage stood.

Hurrying toward it, G.W. saw how the cottage blended with its surroundings. It was one story high, about thirty feet in length, with a thatched roof and a stone chimney from which there was no smoke.

"Odd," G.W. said, "on a chilly afternoon like this."

"Something's not right here, G.W. Do you sense it too?"

A garden planted in front of the cottage had several rows of shriveled plants. The path leading from the front door around the far side of the cottage was covered in leaves no one had swept in days.

G.W. warned, "Take it slow, Sam. I don't like the looks of things."

Stepping cautiously across the weed-filled clearing, Samson approached the west side of the cottage, sniffed the air, and signaled G.W. with his head to come quietly.

G.W. hurried to Samson where he crouched under a window. "Do you see anything?"

Samson shook his head, crept to the front, and cautiously peeked around. G.W. came up behind him. "Don't think anyone's been here for awhile."

Edging around the corner, Samson leapt onto the porch. The front door hung open a few inches. He wedged through and disappeared inside. In moments, he stuck his head out. "No one's home. The fire hasn't been lit for several days, maybe over a week, and the room smells stale."

G.W. climbed the porch steps, pushed open the door, and looked around the disheveled interior. A chair was shoved away from the table and a faded quilt was rumpled on the bed. Several cupboard doors were open and two dirty cups and plates sat in the washbasin. Next to the door, the pegs where cloaks would hang were empty. Only a very old pair of boots stood on the mat.

"What do you make of this?" G.W. asked, holding a man's shirt with the tail torn off.

"Could mean anything," Samson replied as he sniffed along the floor where the smells were strongest. He lifted his nose to G.W. "I'm catching two distinct smells, a man and a girl."

"If I had a better idea where exactly we are in Finnis Fews, I'd be more certain, but it does seem likely this is the girl's home. The cottage looks like the one in my dreams." G.W. moved toward the door. "It worries me she isn't here. Let's check outside. See if we can find some clues."

Samson pushed past G.W. and ran around the cottage to the woodlot. He skidded to a halt and the fur rose on his back. He growled.

Warned, G.W. drew her wand and held it out toward the gouged ground and splintered woodpile. Quickly, she wove the Spell for Revelation. As it filled the area with fog, wavy images drifted across— several rough men attacked another man who had been chopping wood; a blinding, bright flash; the same rough men carrying a heavy log into the woods; and all disappear.

More images formed—a distraught girl, a very large raven, and a huge flock of ravens. In the last image, the girl ran into the woods with a tall dark figure following her.

The Spell of Revelation drained G.W., and she slumped onto a fallen log. Samson climbed into her lap and they rested together. G.W. stroked the cat's thick, orange fur. "An unusual scene, I must say."

"What was that sudden bright light? It was intense. Felt like a wave of evil."

G.W. scratched Samson's chin and set him on the ground. Walking across the woodlot, she pointed to a scorched place in the dirt. "Here's where the blast happened." She sniffed the air and frowned. "It was caused by a twisted kind of magic. It's not the kind I was taught, but I've heard stories about it. It hasn't been known in this world for, I don't know, eons."

She knelt on one knee in the rough dirt and ran her hand over the soil. Her fingers tingled as though shocked. "Sam, whatever happened here must be connected to the attack in the woods. I'm sensing there's evil growing all around the northland. It's no longer a rumor." She shivered. "We've got to find the girl before this evil can catch her."

Nose to the ground, Samson stopped at a dark spot near the chopping block. "Blood, and recent."

As she paced toward the edge of the woodlot, G.W. gleaned what information she could from the scuffed area. When Samson sneezed, she looked up.

"Ravens. Lots of them, and the girl's with them."

G.W. said, "Any way to know why they were here, or what they had to do with the girl?" She paused. "Could they be connected to the blood by the chopping block?"

"I don't see how." He knew birds would peck you for no reason, but he didn't sense they had anything to do with the attack on the man.

"You could be right." G.W. gazed into the dark forest. "Let's get moving, Sami boy. The girl has a good head start. Danger is closing around her faster than we imagined."

Samson's nose tingled with the many smells he'd picked up in the woodlot. When he caught a strong whiff of the girl's scent, he dashed between the trees and disappeared.

Overhead, from where he'd been sitting on a tree branch, the large raven who had followed them since their battle with the FireIce lifted into the sky and headed north.

While his voice remained paralyzed, Anvyartach stayed in bed, gesturing wildly at the slaves. Once they provided what he wanted—food, drink, pillows—they edged out of sight, fearful of this new version of their terrible Master.

Oblivious to their fear, Anvyartach mulled over his newest

revelation. Voiceless did not mean helpless, and the glimpses he had of the girl set his greed on fire. *How do I reach into her mind and force her to come to me? How do I get Mangred to bring the woodcutter—her father, I'm sure of this—here faster? They're connected, and I'll soon make one of them reveal the Key!*

19

G.W. AND SAMSON FOLLOWED the path north from the cottage. Samson raced ahead, his fur bristling. Leaves on the bushes were wilted, their surfaces sickly yellow and rotting.

The air was so thick it was difficult to breathe.

Samson glanced over his shoulder every few seconds. "We're a few days behind them," he said when he caught sight of G.W. puffing along the trail. "Their scent is weak, but it hasn't disappeared."

G.W. rested her back against a sickly beech. She took out a small bowl from an outside pocket, poured water into it, and set it on the ground in front of Samson.

He lapped at the water before asking, "Does your magic help you read who's been through here? Mine senses something is damaged inside the trees."

G.W.'s eyes glazed for a moment and her wand slipped from under her cloak into her hand. Touching the trunk with a delicate flick, G.W. flinched as though shocked. "They're suffering with a deep fear, like—" She paused, their trauma was so distressing. "Like they've borne an unimaginable pain."

Samson tilted his head and his whiskers quivered. "This can't be good."

G.W. continued through the trees, laying her wand on their trunks. Her shoulders slumped farther with each new touch.

Concerned by G.W.'s growing distraction, Samson blurted his own worries. "I've caught the smell of something worse—that black ooze isn't far from here."

The mention of the ooze stopped G.W. "There's never a good time to run into that again."

"I can smell it. Not as strong, but it's here. Makes my whiskers throb."

G.W. sniffed the air. An unpleasant smell wafted around her, not exactly the same as the ooze but definitely repulsive. Tucking the wand back into her cloak, she reached for the cat. "Let me hold you a minute, Orange Boy. You have a way of calming my nerves." The cat's purr vibrated through his body.

After several good scratches behind his ears and under his chin, G.W. said, "I've noticed something else." She set the cat on the forest floor and gazed into the treetops. "Since leaving the cottage, have you seen any animals or heard any birds overhead?"

"Now that you mention it, these woods are strangely silent. We're chasing something that has terrified both the vegetation and the wildlife."

G.W. squatted next to Samson and whispered, "Don't move, Warrior." It was the prearranged code for imminent danger. "We're being watched." She lifted her eyebrows to indicate the direction of her thoughts.

On alert, Samson flattened his whiskers against his face and flicked the end of his tail. A deep rumble built in his throat and erupted as a piercing yowl just as a horde of hairy beasts the size of giant bears rushed at them.

Fiery bolts from G.W.'s wand landed on the thick fur of the nearest beasts. They yelped but kept moving toward her. They stood on heavy legs, their heads covered in dark, matted hair. Yellow eyes squinted under thick eyebrows. Sharp teeth jutted from wide, open mouths. Arms reached below their knees, and their hands and fingers were covered in scraggly hair. They attacked with bloodthirsty screams.

In a blur of rage, Samson leapt, claws unsheathed, razor sharp fangs ready to sink into the beast's hide. His claws slashed the beast's face. It yowled and grabbed too late for the attacker. The forest filled with shrieks each time Samson's claws caught an unprotected face or hand. Blood flew from the cat's berserk assaults. Flames burst from G.W.'s wand into the massive assailants, scorching their fur and setting more than one matted head on fire.

Victory, however, went to Kellach, the leader of the WilderOnes, whose enormous club felled both the old wizardess and the cat. His yellow teeth snapped as drool fell from his mouth. The beasts growled at the captives.

"Bring them," barked Kellach as he disappeared down the trail.

Skawhok and Hawken, who had suffered most, kicked each captive for good measure. Hawken, the burlier of the two, lifted the woman and threw her over his shoulder while Skawhok grabbed the cat and tried to stuff him into his burlap bag. Samson sank his teeth into the thick matt of hair that covered Skawhok's arm, but the putrid taste sickened the cat so much he puked on his captor.

"Yeow!" screamed Skawhok as he threw the cat to the ground. Before Samson could stand on his wobbly legs, Skawhok grabbed him around the middle and squeezed. "Try that again and you'll be paste!"

Samson was squashed and kicked and thrown several more times before he was finally stuffed into his captor's sack. The stench of Skawhok's body made him retch again. Skawhok thumped the bag with his balled fist.

G.W.'s wand caught in the folds of her cloak when she was clubbed. As Hawken threw her over his shoulder, her arms dangled down his back and her cape was pinned under her where she couldn't reach the wand. She was dizzy from the blows the creatures had landed, and each breath was a stab of pain.

As Hawken and Skawhok lumbered through the woods, other eyes watched them. Overhead Brand'oo circled, careful to stay out of their sight. Making a thorough reconnaissance of the area, the raven noted the WilderOnes camp and raced away.

Much later, G.W. opened one eye and squinted at her surroundings. She lay on a soft pillow that groaned.

"Shhhhh," G.W. whispered to Samson's foot.

"Gr-grrrr-sfumaeplet dftt pht," the cat mumbled in a language unknown to anyone.

G.W. kept her eyes closed as long as possible, in case one of the monstrous beasts was watching. When she risked a glance, she saw nothing but dirt in front, dirt underneath, and pebbles near her hand. She listened for another minute. The only sounds she recognized were Samson's muffled breathing and her own gasps for air. If the hairy one who'd knocked her down and kicked her and tossed her over his shoulder was nearby, she couldn't see him.

She whispered in a ragged voice, "Don't move a muscle, Sam. These thugs are ruthless." G.W. couldn't see Kellach sleeping against a rock twenty feet away, waiting for the others to return with enough wood to make a roaring fire on which to roast their captives.

"I think they've left us alone, but in case I'm wrong, let's get out of here while they think we're still unconscious." She inched her hand across the dirt. "When I signal, race for the woods."

No word came from the burlap bag, but Samson wriggled stealthily until his front paws were out. He took a deep breath and pulled the rest of his body forward. When he was almost clear, G.W. shouted, "NOW!"

The orange cat erupted from beneath her. His fur stood straight out from his body. He shrieked like a million demons had exploded into the WilderOneses' clearing. G.W. grabbed her pack and sprinted for the safety of the woods. "RUN!"

Kellach was so startled by the orange creature's fury he couldn't move for a moment, but he recovered quickly, shook his giant head, and roared. The colossal WilderOne grabbed his club and stomped toward the escapees. In three lunging steps, Kellach would have caught both of them, but before he could take two steps, his head was caught in a storm of wings, sharp claws, and piercing beaks aimed at his eyes. Kellach bellowed and swung his club in all directions, but the attackers were too quick and darted out of reach, only to return at lightning speed from another direction aiming at the most vulnerable spots on his body.

Hearing their leader's roar, the scavenging WilderOnes raced back to the camp where a flock of large, angry ravens met them. The birds harried them, battering their heads and bodies with powerful wings and beaks.

Bewildered by the onslaught, the WilderOnes swung their clubs at the birds, but their swings were awkward and most often they walloped each other. Swinging their clubs wildly, Hawken and Skawhok became entangled in each other's spiky vests, fell to the ground, and, blinded by fearsome beaks, rolled and clawed and gouged each other, each certain he was battling a monster.

Kellach, dizzy from swinging his enormous club at the whirling birds, tripped over his feet and fell with a great *Whoosh!*, striking his head on a large rock. He slumped like a sack of broken eggs. Seeing their leader knocked to the ground, perhaps dead, the cowardly pack of WilderOnes shrieked and scattered in all directions, their only thought to escape the fury of the terrifying attackers.

As quickly as the battle had begun, it ended. The ravens disappeared over the trees, except for Brand'oo who swooped overhead and watched for signs of returning attackers. When he was satisfied the immediate threat was over, the raven lifted into the air to search for the woman and the cat.

G.W. pushed through the dense underbrush putting as much distance between her and those beasts as possible. She called to

Samson. "Where are you, Orange Boy?" She tripped, righted herself, and shoved on through the woods. Her legs trembled, her breath came in ragged gasps, and her head felt as though it would explode. "I have to rest. If I don't, I'll wander forever and never find him." She dropped where she was and commanded her tired brain: *Think!*

Despair filled her heart. G.W.'s backpack wriggled. An impossible sound came from deep inside—the unmistakable rumbling of a purr.

"Oh, you beautiful cat!" she cried as Samson gingerly pulled himself from the backpack. He looked as though he'd been wrung out, hung by his ears to dry, and tossed into a briar patch. Patches of his thick, orange fur were pulled out and sticks and leaves covered him, but he was alive.

"Ouch!" he said as G.W. tried to hug him. "I think I've been skinned and my fur reattached inside out."

"You poor thing." G.W. was careful not to touch him anywhere except the tips of his ears. "Let me examine you. My medicines and my wand are here somewhere. Did you ever see an uglier bunch of brutes? They were planning to roast us for dinner!"

G.W. rattled on. The realization they'd escaped a fate too hideous to think about nearly made her weep. "You may not have noticed, Orange Jewel, but we're lost."

"Did I make this part up," Samson asked, "or did a flock of enormous birds attack those beasts?"

"I never saw anything like it," G.W. said. "Ravens by the score dropped out of the sky and made mincemeat out of them. Wish I knew where they went."

Before she finished, G.W. heard the flapping of silky wings.

"Right here."

A glossy raven landed on the nearest branch and was followed by another, and another, and another until the trees filled with the shimmering iridescence of Fial and his troop of ravens.

20

"WELL, THIS IS A FINE GATHERING," G.W. said as she stared at the largest group of ravens she'd ever seen. By her side, Samson snarled. Birds made him nervous.

"We aren't here to harm you, cat. Quite the opposite." Fial hopped toward the two. "If you're able to move, we'd best go before those brutes wake up. They'll be outraged and wanting revenge."

Without waiting for a response, Fial leapt into the air. "Brave birds, away!"

The congress of ravens lifted into the sky and sped off.

All disappeared except Brand'oo, who swept down in front of G.W. and Samson. "Follow me."

Hours later, Brand'oo swooped close to G.W. "It's just a few more steps, in the clearing by the giant firs."

Gratefully, G.W. trudged toward the raven-filled trees. She eased the pack from her shoulders and knelt beside it. "Come out, Orange Pie. Easy does it."

When Samson emerged, G.W. grimaced. "My, you have been playing with the big boys."

Her tension eased as she tended the cat's cuts and bruises. She made Samson a warm drink and added a few drops of healing tonic. As he lapped it up, the cat's familiar purr returned.

Guilt, however, filled Samson's mind. *I should have finished off that last brute. Instead, I dashed after G.W. and burrowed into her knapsack. Escaping from the creatures wasn't so terrible,* he reasoned, *but to be outdone by birds! How could any self-respecting cat get over that?*

Overhead, sitting away from the others, one raven stared at the cat. She repeatedly ruffled the feathers on her head and puffed out the ruff around her neck in a fearsome way.

"Shoo! Get out of here!" Samson hissed.

The bird hopped sideways but continued to stare.

"Maybe you don't know this," Samson said, "but cats love nothing more than raven pie for breakfast."

The bird hopped onto Samson's back and pecked him.

"Ow! Stop it!"

"Then stop making such disagreeable sounds, Cat."

Samson was unused to talking with birds. His inability to save his best friend G.W. weighed heavily on his conscience.

"I see you're able to understand Raven," Biab said. "Maybe you'll learn something useful if you listen." Her *tok-tok-tok* in his ear was clear as a bell.

Biab hopped back to her perch, her black eyes glittering. Her throat ruff spread out fully, and Samson recognized the dignity of this winged creature.

"You'd make a lovely mouthful, though," he said and immediately regretted it as she descended on him in a whirring mass of feathers.

"Cat, you're a fine lump of fur. Why didn't you save your friend back there?"

Samson growled but her taunt shamed him. "I don't know. I just didn't. Drop it, will you? Leave me alone!"

Biab hopped around him, tilting her head sideways and considering him from every angle. Finally she said, "Maybe you should say thank you."

Samson stared at her.

"If it hadn't been for Brand'oo, we would never have been able to rescue you in time. He's the one who deserves your gratitude." She stepped closer to the cat. "The moment he saw those creatures, he took wing and didn't rest until he'd found us. Didn't stop until he'd convinced Fial to follow him."

This remarkable act dumbfounded Samson. A bird had taken extreme measures to help him and G.W.? Straightening up, he asked, "Where is he? I do want to thank him."

"Sleeping. And nursing his wing."

"He's wounded?" Samson laid his head down on his paws. Useless.

G.W.'s comforting hands lifted him gently. "Who's your friend, Sam? I want to thank her and the others for rescuing us. We'd be roast meat if they hadn't showed up when they did."

Biab winked at Samson as if to say, "Ah, hah! At last someone with manners."

After Biab introduced herself and told the tale of Brand'oo's bravery, G.W. lifted her arm in a grand salute and bowed. "How can we ever thank you for your brave and selfless rescue and for bringing us to safety?"

"No need, Wise One. You're new to this part of the forest, are you not? We want to hear how you and the cat came to be in Finnis Fews, but this is a story everyone needs to hear. Come meet the others."

The paralysis of Anvyartach's voice gradually eased. One moment he couldn't utter a word; the next he was screaming at the poor slave who'd dropped his shoe. "Imbecile!"

The word came out loud and clear. He had spoken. Shocked, the sullen Shadow Lord stopped his hand midair. "Imbecile! Imbecile!"

Thrilled, Anvyartach danced around the room, holding the limp slave by the arms. "You are an imbecile!" he laughed and gave him a clout that sent him spinning.

Anvyartach had never felt so good. His voice had returned, his powers were growing, and nothing would stop him from finding the Key. "Mangred, I've watched your pathetic progress through the forest too long. Why are you dawdling when I need to speak to that child's father?"

In the library, Anvyartach kicked fallen books as he ran his fingers along the shelves searching for the one with the special spell to send his voice through space. He grabbed a dislodged book. It fell open in his hand. He stopped breathing. The words shimmered.

> *Weep, oh, incompetent mages.*
> *The secrets of Far Speaking are herein revealed,*
> *Yet the answers are beyond your command.*
> *Understanding will be a cap of confusion,*
> *Words an impenetrable, tangled maze.*
> *The door to knowledge is bolted to all but the brilliant few.*
> *Quit now.*
> *You will fail, like all before you.*

The dread words sank into Anvyartach's mind. Anger and fear battled for control. "I'm not one of *those* magicians. I am a First Creator. My powers are beyond any ever known in this miserable world. I will know your secrets."

Anvyartach poured over the ancient spell, calling up knowledge from long ago when he had been one of the ruling creators of Idelisia. Arcane words and phrases baffled his still developing brain, but gradually their hidden meanings grew clearer. The mystery of Far Speaking was within his grasp.

Too impatient to translate every word, Anvyartach grabbed the ancient book and hurried to his laboratory. "The ingredients must all be there somewhere. I just need to be a bit more careful than last time." He rubbed his throat absently.

Bumping open the door to the laboratory with one hip, Anvyartach rushed forward. "Once I can control my speech with Mangred and that girl, the prisoner's knowledge will be mine. He will reveal where my Key is hidden. I'll tell Mangred how to force it out of him."

Anvyartach hurried to the shelves to collect the necessary ingredients, shoving bottles and vials into his arms next to the book. The next instant, his incomplete hip crumpled. Anvyartach crashed to the floor. The precious book flew from his grasp as liquid and powdered ingredients mixed in choking confusion.

"AIEEEE!"

When the Shadow Lord tried to rise, his left leg refused to bend. Instead, it buckled, throwing him back down onto the floor. This time his heavy black robe tangled around his neck and bound one arm close to his body. Unable to right himself, Anvyartach inched across the floor searching for the precious book that contained the secret of Far Speaking.

The book had skittered under a tall wooden cabinet that rested on short legs. "Ah-hah! There you are." He poked his free arm beneath it. His hand chose that moment to lock his fingers into a stiff mitt and refuse to work. "No, no, no! Not now!"

Tantalizingly close, the book remained just out of reach. Anvyartach concentrated all his energy on his hands and panted, "I—can—get—it."

Sensation gradually returned to his hands. Fueled by impatience, Anvyartach heaved his body against the cabinet, lifting it enough to get closer to the book. Glass vials rattled inside the cabinet as they slid into each other. The book remained just out of reach.

Anvyartach took a deep breath and gave a mighty push. The heavy cabinet rocked precariously, wobbled a moment, and fell with a deafening crash. When the dust settled, the Shadow Lord wiped his mouth and squinted. The book, buried somewhere under the rubble of broken glass and splintered wood, had disappeared.

A chilling howl echoed around the room as Anvyartach tore into the wreckage. His arms quivered from the exertion and his knees ached. His robe and face were covered in the fine dust of decayed paper and splintered wood. Debris flew everywhere.

"I've got you!" he barked when he glimpsed the flattened book. Fearful it might disintegrate if he pulled too hard, he picked up the precious book and held it to his chest.

Anvyartach sobbed with relief and sank back against the fallen cabinet. "Oh, you beautiful thing."

21

PRRUK-PRRUK-PRRUK!

Startled by the warning call, Fial leapt into the air from the branches of the fir tree and circled the camp. When he spied the source of the call several emotions flashed through him: relief there was no real danger, irritation such a warning had been given for such a trivial matter, and no surprise at all.

Biab was playing catch-me-if-you-can with the big, orange cat. The cat's sharp claws slashed at the nimble bird whose metallic *prruk-prruks* inflamed the cat further. Each time Samson surged up to grab Biab from the air, she slipped away at the last moment, shook her shaggy throat feathers, and laughed.

"Big Orange Fluff Ball! Can't catch me!" she taunted as she made maddening circles over his head.

True cat that he was, Samson chased Biab until he wobbled dizzily and fell on his side.

Although the game was over, Samson watched the irreverent bird as he licked his side, his legs, and his paws while flexing his claws.

Fial settled to the ground near Samson. "Don't mind her. She

likes to tease everyone until they're too dizzy or too angry to continue. No one's beat her yet so she's quite sure of herself."

Finishing his bath with apparent nonchalance, Samson mumbled, "Next time she may get a surprise."

Fial didn't doubt that Biab had found a worthy opponent. Nodding, Fial glanced over his shoulder and saw G.W. resting with her back against a large beech tree.

"Your furry companion has a lot of patience. Biab may not get away so easily next time."

G.W. laughed. "That orange fur ball has a few tricks even I don't know about."

"I'd like to hear your story," Fial said, "if you're ready to tell it."

G.W. stared into the raven's eyes. "We come from a place called OneHome, many miles west of this great forest. Finnis Fews has been a mystery to my people until—" She hesitated. She knew so little about this raven and his clan and was uncertain what she could safely say.

Fial stared at her, waiting for her to continue. When G.W. remained silent, he barked the gathering call. *Cark! Cark!*

As iridescent birds flocked around their leader, G.W. made her way to sit next to Samson. She pulled the cat onto her lap, where he squirmed in embarrassment.

The ravens circled their leader. With no warning, Fial whirled in a cloud of sparkling dust and rose to his full human form. G.W. had never seen such a remarkable transformation. Samson remained rigid on her lap, his tail twitching.

Fial's black cape swirled around him, the stars twinkling along its folds as it settled against his ankles. He lifted his chin slightly, a regal pose, and surveyed his band. "Friends! New dangers have invaded our land, but they haven't reached us yet."

Beaks clacked and feathers rustled.

"Recently, we've had many challenges. First the girl wanting to find her missing father, and now these two who have struggled with the WilderOnes. Nor can we forget the attack of the black ooze, the most powerful enemy we've faced yet."

Nervous wing whistles filled the air.

"Add the mysterious threat in the north who is gathering his strength. If not stopped, he will destroy our world."

The ravens shuddered.

"I only wish we had found Oelsa sooner. We might have been able to save her father."

G.W. and Samson looked at each other. "Fial," G.W. said, "forgive my interruption, but what girl?"

"A child we met recently. I found her near a cottage in the middle of Finnis Fews."

"How long ago?"

"Why do you ask? Do you know something about the girl or her father?"

"I ask because we also seek a special child, one whose heart shines from within. We both dreamed of her and the danger surrounding her. We've been racing to find her before she and her light are extinguished."

G.W. was greeted by a flurry of flapping wings and ruffled neck feathers.

"Silence!" Fial shouted to the birds before turning back to G.W. "What do you know about the threat against her?"

G.W. touched Samson's back, and he leapt from her lap. When

she moved to the center of the gathered ravens, Samson stretched to his full height, and with the dignity of an ancient deity, placed himself directly in front of her.

"My people tell an old story about the creation of our world," G.W. began in a low voice. She glanced around the circle of birds and continued. "When all was completed, not one inch, not one branch, not one berry was ill-formed. All was perfect."

The gravity in G.W.'s tone riveted their attention.

"But the First Creators made one significant mistake," G.W. said. "In their desire to create a perfect, idyllic home, they overlooked, or perhaps simply ignored, a basic principle at our core—the need for balance. They failed to recognize perfection is, at best, boring, and, at worst, destructive. For all the uplifting, beautiful, easy elements of life to be fully appreciated, their opposites must also be acknowledged."

She paused. The ravens remained silent, the weight of the words sinking in. Fial stood to the side, arms folded across his chest, scowling.

"In time, some among the First Creators rebelled against the sterile sameness. Perfection was wearisome. They yearned for something more stimulating. What they didn't expect was the addictive nature of destruction, and soon these rebels couldn't stop. Negative energy consumed them until the only acceptable outcome became the annihilation of their flawless world."

The ravens listened with rapt attention. "Anvyartach," G.W. said, "the Shadow Lord, led a war against the First Creators and almost succeeded. His ambition eclipsed any decency or moderation he might once have had. He came to believe he deserved to be the one, indisputable Supreme Ruler."

The ravens shivered as G.W. wove the story.

"If Anvyartach had succeeded, Idelisia would have been shattered, and all would have been subject to the Shadow Lord's cruelty."

A tear fell down G.W.'s cheek. "He nearly triumphed. Had it not been for my many-greats grandmother, Nuala, he would have succeeded. The girl in Samson's and my dreams carries the power to save Idelisia from another such attack."

Biab glanced at Fial. G.W.'s words confirmed his earlier message.

G.W. cleared her throat and lowered her voice as though the enemy might be listening from the dark forest. "The gift she has is both delicate and all-powerful. The fact that she is completely unaware of this Key she carries has kept her safe until now."

The ravens rocked uneasily on the tree branches. They had never before heard of such a Key. Fial grasped his cloak more tightly. "Tell us more, G.W."

"Idelisia's enemy was scattered atom by atom throughout the universe, but he has managed to re-form himself. His power grows. He intends to become the Supreme Ruler of Idelisia. He believes he can wrest the Key from the girl before she discovers her power. When he has what he wants, he will kill her."

The warning chilled them. None, except Fial, had realized the ominous consequences of their failure to save the girl.

"We must find her," G.W. said. "Samson and I are certain that without her we are all doomed. We must do everything we can to help her discover how to use her gift before Anvyartach finds her."

Biab stood and shook out her feathers. "How do you know it's the same girl we met in the Heart of the Woods?"

"It is a fair question," G.W. said. "If we are correct, she can trace her lineage to the First Creators. After Anvyartach failed to destroy the First Creators' world, this girl's family was chosen to carry the Key that would repel any future attack. Perhaps you are wondering why her ancestors were given this overwhelming responsibility?"

The ravens nervously shifted positions along their branches. Fial nodded.

"Because, my friends, they are Anvyartach's family."

The only sound was the breeze lifting the leaves in the oak trees.

"I mentioned that Nuala helped to destroy Anvyartach's power, an overwhelming task," G.W. said, "especially because Anvyartach was her husband."

The gathered raven clan gasped.

"Their lives had been blessed with children they loved. Nuala was one of the First Creators and Anvyartach's equal. When he turned toward the dark, she begged him to listen to his heart, to his wife, and to their beloved children. She pleaded with him not to destroy their lives, their love, but his heart had hardened and he would not listen.

"Once Anvyartach was defeated and the punishment decreed, Nuala vowed she would never allow such a disaster to happen again. She had loved Anvyartach with her heart and soul, and her failure to turn him back to the light nearly destroyed her. Because she had failed, she vowed she would stop at nothing to guarantee this would never happen again.

"Nuala devoted the rest of her life to the creation of the greatest power Idelisia had ever known, and to finding a way to keep it hidden until it was needed. When she at last succeeded, she gave the Key to her youngest daughter, along with the instructions on how to pass it from generation to generation, mother to daughter, into eternity.

"No one believed Anvyartach would ever return, and the secret of the Key was revealed only as the bearer neared the end of her life. Oelsa's father knew the secret because his wife told him before she died, but no urgency was attached to the secret. Anvyartach had been gone for eons. Everyone believed his return was impossible."

Biab hopped toward G.W. "But how are you and the girl connected? Surely a dream isn't enough to bring you into Finnis Fews so far from your home."

"Little raven, you are right. A dream, by itself, would not have compelled Samson and me to leave OneHome." She swallowed. "Oelsa is my granddaughter."

Samson rubbed against her legs.

Biab broke the silence. "I will go with you and the cat to find her."

G.W. smiled at the courageous raven.

Fial took a deep breath and said, "Let the clan respond to this brave—and rash—offer by our friend Biab. Do you wish to see her go?"

No response.

"Do you wish to join her?"

The ravens erupted into a tumult of flapping wings, clacking bills, and raucous croaking voices. "We do!"

Fial lifted his arms. "Raven Clan, you make me proud to be your leader!"

22

ANVYARTACH SCREAMED when the ingredients for the Far Speaking spell ran over the top of the glass vial. Making the spell had been a disaster. "How many times do I have to do this?" He wrenched the vial from its holder and threw it against the wall where it shattered atop a growing pile of broken shards.

"It's that pea-brained woodcutter's fault! And Mangred's! If he weren't so lazy, he'd have delivered that moron to me by now!"

Anvyartach grabbed another glass vial and jammed it into the clamp on the workbench next to the directions. "Once more. I can do this once more." Anvyartach pawed through the many vials spread in front of him.

For the last several days, the Shadow Lord had attempted to make the arcane formula, but despite his most careful attention, something always went wrong. The concoction exploded with the last drop, or the ingredients turned into a gelatinous glop.

"Why does it always fail?" he howled, as the mixture he was so carefully swirling turned green and oozed over the top of the vial.

"Mangred! Bring that worthless woodcutter to me NOW!"

Knowing his henchman couldn't hear him enraged Anvyartach even more, and he stomped about the room, kicking books out of his way, waving his arms, barely stopping before he swept the precious magical powders from the table.

"Maybe she's the only one I need. It's her mind I've touched." He stopped to consider this possibility. "I not only heard her, I saw her. That's it! I need her! I'll make her believe I have her father and she'll fly to me."

Malicious laughter poured from the Shadow Lord. "If Mangred delivers her father here first, he'll give me the answer I need. But if I succeed with the Far Speaking potion, I can invade her mind any time I want!"

His hands shook with frustration, but a new confidence filled his black heart. "I glimpsed her mind once. I can do it again." He set to remaking the same potion that had given him access to the girl's mind, this time following all the instructions to the last detail. "When I control her mind, the secret of the Key will be mine!"

Mangred struggled to pull his boot out of the muddy track. "Radjit rauferin' frugg ruts," he growled. "This is all I need, this endless mud." Steam rose from his leather vest as he strained to take another step. Behind him, the soldiers carrying the captured woodcutter stopped, the weight of the prisoner's log dragging them down into the bottomless mud.

Stuck under Mangred's shoulder strap, Velvet lay useless. He studied the edges of the muddy pit, searching for something strong enough. "That branch should do nicely."

Weariness turned his arms to lead, but Mangred only needed to envision Anvyartach's rage to goad him to action. Pulling the whip from under the strap, he eyed the distance between himself and the stout branch. With one careful snap of the whip, he wrapped it around the branch, tugged it tight, and used it as leverage to pull himself out of the muck. Digging his elbows into the bank, he crawled the last few feet until he felt a satisfying "pop." He dragged himself free and collapsed.

As soon as he caught his breath, Mangred unwrapped Velvet from the branch, kissed it shamelessly, and edged toward the soldiers where they had sunk up to their knees in the mire. Getting the first soldier to hold on to the whip took vicious threats, but finally one man wrapped Velvet around his wrist and held fast as Mangred tugged him free. Seeing their friend pulled free, the others begged to be next.

"NO! The log comes next," Mangred roared.

Three of the mud bound soldiers wrestled the whip around the log.

"Push, you lazy dogs! Heave it toward me!" Mangred called them every name he could think of until eventually the log slithered onto solid ground.

It took another hour to free the remaining men. Once on solid ground, they sprawled where they had landed and refused to move.

Inside the log, Dahvi floated in a sap-filled dream world, unaware of the fate toward which he was being carried.

"Have some water," Ardreas urged Oelsa. The path they were following was little more than an animal's track. He slipped off his pack and set it on the ground.

Convincing her to follow him had been challenging. She clung to the idea their best chance to rescue her father was to continue eastward, in hopes of finding the Tower of Kedric. But Ardreas was certain they were more likely to find her father if they intercepted his kidnappers. He admitted to himself this was guesswork, but a calculated risk was better than blundering blindly through the impenetrable forest, especially considering the all-too-real possibility this Tower was no more than a myth, a fiction invented by the First Creators to mask their near failure.

Ardreas also worried about the girl's attitude. She halted often and her eyes glazed over, as though she were focusing on something miles away. Whenever he asked her to explain, Oelsa said vaguely, "Never mind. I thought I heard something."

When Oelsa took the leather flask, Ardreas flinched as though he'd been poked with a stick, and a sudden urge to find his brother Owen gripped him. The compulsion to search right now was irresistible. "Stay right there, Oelsa," he called to her. "It's Owen. He needs me. Stay on the path and don't move!"

Before she could respond, Ardreas disappeared into the dark woods.

Surprised, Oelsa leaned against a hazel tree. "What's gotten into him?" she asked a squirrel who was staring at her. She sipped the cool water, wet the corner of her cloak, and rubbed it across her hot face. Refreshed, she settled on the ground, pulled her knees up to her chest, wrapped her arms around them, and yawned. "I hope he isn't gone too long."

The next thing she knew, a familiar voice was in her head.

"I know where he is, girl." Anvyartach's oily tone wheedled into her mind.

Oelsa leapt up and looked up and down the gloomy path.

The voice continued. "He needs you, girl. Listen to me and I will take you to him."

"To Ardreas?"

"To your father."

"Who are you?"

Menacing laughter filled her head. "I thought you'd be interested, girl. Your father is here with me. He needs you. Follow my voice and I will lead you to him."

Oelsa fought against the overwhelming urge to step into the dark forest. Every ounce of her body warned: Do not leave the path. Ardreas said to wait here.

But the voice was irresistible. "Your poor father is begging you to come to him."

The words ate into Oelsa's will and eroded her better judgment. "Father! Are you there?"

She was torn between the yearning to find him and Ardreas's directions to stay where she was. "Where have you gone, Ardreas? Why haven't you come back?"

When Ardreas did not respond, Oelsa's resolve broke, and she plunged into the forest as though hypnotized. *I will follow the voice, Father. It will lead me to you*, she thought. She raced into the woods away from where Ardreas expected to find her.

An hour later Ardreas returned. "Oelsa, I'm back. Owen was nowhere to be found. I don't know why I thought he was right there."

Oelsa wasn't there. He ran another twenty feet, but she didn't answer his calls. Ardreas turned back and shouted her name. He spied his water flask on the ground. "Oh, no! She's done the unthinkable—she's gone off, alone, into that jumble of trees. OELSA!"

Oelsa ran without thinking. She pushed her way through the towering oaks and brushed against the bark of an old hemlock. Boughs whipped her cheeks, but she couldn't stop. The voice in her head sounded more and more like her father's. He was calling her. The more she ran, the more certain she became that he was just ahead.

"Father, wait!"

Ardreas paced back and forth. "Which way would she have gone?"

His concern for Oelsa overrode the odd and compelling certainty he'd felt earlier that Owen needed him.

A chime rang like the ghost of a word or half-finished thought. "Odd," Ardreas said. "I've never heard such a sound in these parts."

The next chime slipped under Ardreas's skin like tiny feet in silk slippers. Wisps of sound worked their way deeper and deeper into his mind, sinking into his vanishing consciousness. He dropped to his knees and fell face down.

A host of black beetles sprang from the forest floor and crawled over his head, down his back, and out along his arms and legs. Chattering excitedly, they swarmed Ardreas's body, their minuscule legs and feelers and wings pulsing. The minds of innumerable insects throbbed with their leader's command: Bring him to the great mound.

The deeper into the woods Oelsa went, the more desperate she became. Mindless of the scratches on her face and arms or the tears to her blue cloak, Oelsa plunged on. When she paused, her father's words goaded her forward. "Help me! Hurry!"

Sobbing, Oelsa pushed against spruce branches that touched the forest floor. When she tried to push past them, she couldn't. "Let go of me!" As she thrashed against them, the realization hit her: *I should never have left the path where Ardreas said to wait.*

A rank odor drifted through the trees, far away, probing, testing, hunting for the one distinct scent it craved more than any other.

The spell finally worked. Anvyartach was thrilled. He sank onto the cold throne and wiped the sweat from his face. "Two in one go! The girl and the other one, the one the beetles have captured!" He snorted with pleasure. "Too bad I can't watch what those nasty insects will do to the man." He cackled and rubbed his hands together.

"The girl is under my power at last, following my voice." The force of the Far Speaking burned in his mind even as it eroded his energy. "Mangred will find her. She must be close to him." He couldn't keep his eyes open. "Mangred will pay, of course, for the bungling of the woodcutter's arrival, but the girl is much easier to manipulate. I'll deal with Mangred . . . later . . . he'll suffer . . ."

Ardreas awoke somewhere underground. Unsure if he had opened his eyes—the room was so dark—he tried to sit up, but his arms and legs were weighed down. He surveyed his body, but all seemed unharmed. *So why can't I move?*

Lights flared in the cavern, momentarily blinding Ardreas. As his eyes adjusted, a sparkling mosaic of the shining backs of ten thousand beetles in an infinite variety of sizes and colors spread across the domed ceiling. Amazed by their diversity and complex patterns, Ardreas whispered, "Where am I? Paradise?"

A booming voice filled the cavern. "You think this is paradise?"

Laughter from the thousands of beetles surged through the cavern.

"Silence!" boomed the deep voice coming from high overhead, hidden in the darkness. "You are far from paradise, intruder!"

A host of beetles pushed against Ardreas, stinging his arms. Drops of poison worked into his blood. "Stop that! I'm no intruder." He tried to wrench his arms loose, but the poison made his muscles unresponsive. Hundreds of tiny feet crawled over his face, stinging him repeatedly.

"You have intruded into our realm," the menacing voice boomed. "You will pay the price all intruders must pay."

The beetle mob hissed and clicked, their tiny pincers clacking and making a terrible din.

Ardreas had never experienced anything like this before he met the girl. He thought of her with some irritation. *Where did you go? I don't know why I had to find Owen, but surely you could have waited*, he thought. *Wherever you are, I can't help you. I've got my own worries, namely extricating myself from these nasty insects, before whoever owns that venomous voice carries out his threats.*

23

MANGRED RESTED ON A FALLEN LOG and mopped his brow. After the disaster in the mud pit, he had pushed his men harder than ever. His face was red with heat and exertion. At his feet rested the log in which Dahvi was imprisoned. The soldiers sprawled, limp with exhaustion, next to it.

Mangred spit in disgust. "Gutless weaklings." He sneered as he caressed Velvet. But the numbing days of pushing through this pathless wood had weakened even his determination. "Stay there in the dirt, then, you worthless cowards."

Inside the log, Dahvi's conscious mind floated as his body dissolved into the tree's sap. Thoughts drifted in random threads, and he could no longer grasp the meanings of certain words, nor feel any strong emotion. His mind wanted to slip away.

Mangred worried that the longer they wandered in the forest, the less likely the prisoner would be alive by the time they reached Tirvar. Anvyartach had demanded he be delivered alive. "Pick up the log. Stop your bellyaching!"

When only groans rose from the men, Velvet sang over their heads and nipped at their ears until the men staggered to their feet.

"Put your backs into it!"

Anvyartach shivered in his icy palace. Thoughts of Mangred's slow progress ate at him. During the days he had tried to find the secret of creating Far Speaking, Anvyartach had ignored their wandering. Now that he had the secret, he would prod Mangred harder. "You disappoint me, Mangred," he sneered, "but you can still retrieve your miserable life by finding that girl."

Anvyartach snatched the glass orb from the table and rubbed his hands over its surface. "Come on, Mangred. Show yourself."

Mangred's men's struggles with the log slowly came into cloudy view. "I'm on to you, Mangred. I know what you're doing." Unfortunately, the anger sizzling across Anvyartach's mind had an unexpected effect—it burned away the last of the Far Speaking potion. As his power dissipated, he poured all his energy into retrieving the Far Speaking. Only a wisp of energy reached into the glass orb.

Panicked that his powers were disappearing instead of growing, he screamed, again and again, "FIND THE GIRL!"

"Halt!" Mangred commanded. He rubbed his head. "Who said that? Speak up!"

The men cowered and looked at their feet. No one had spoken.

"I know you're lying! Someone just said something about a girl. Confess!" He clutched Velvet. The leather thong snaked in front of their eyes. Before he could unleash its bite, however, Mangred stiffened and looked over his shoulder. "Master? Is that you? Are you talking to me?"

Mangred's fear was unmistakable. "He can't be here. That's impossible. But I just heard him." He sent Velvet singing over the men's heads. "Pick up the log and move, you poor beggars. Run for your lives!"

Anvyartach raced to the laboratory. "Where did I leave that spell? Why did it stop working?" He pushed the heavy door open and froze. The room was as he had left it—cluttered, books dropped from shelves, potion ingredients spilled helter-skelter over the table and floor.

Fighting panic, Anvyartach tore through the debris, desperate to find the one book that held the precious Far Speaking instructions.

Books flew over his head and crashed against the walls. He scoured the worktable, pushing books out of his way, hoping the right book would filter to the top of the mess. Powders sprayed into the air as he swiped at the table top, liquids spilling onto the floor, some sizzling, some burning to the touch. Anvyartach was impervious to all sensations. Madness drove him to tear and throw all in his sight. "Where are you?" he screamed at the mess he was creating.

Finally, exhausted, Anvyartach clutched the edge of the table and panted. Nothing remained on its top. "It has to be here. I left it when I finished the last time." Desperation ate at his gut and caused him to double over. More books were under the table, and he allowed himself to slip down to the floor. "Slower," he told himself. "Take your time."

Several minutes passed as the Shadow Lord rummaged among the heaps of books. He forced himself to stack the books five high, gradually, reading the titles, rubbing his hands over their covers, until, at last, the book he sought fell into his hands. "Yes!" he said, standing abruptly and banging his head on the edge of the hard table.

Setting the book down, he thumbed through the pages until the spell appeared. He read carefully, every detail now renewed, and discovered a line he had missed during his first rush to translate the arcane words: "For long-lasting effect, avoid extreme emotion. Repeated use will increase the potency."

Anvyartach shivered with delight. "Your secret is revealed. I cannot be fooled!"

Step by step, Anvyartach remixed the potion, carefully swirling the ingredients in the vial. "Concentrate," he said and moved down the list of instructions. Finally, the last step was completed and the potion smoked and swirled.

"This time I am to drink it immediately, in one gulp," he said as he swallowed the red concoction. Anvyartach waited. Suppressed rage simmered under his skin. Murderous thoughts threatened to erupt if nothing happened soon.

An intense surge of strength and might infused every atom of his being. Unbidden, fierce words burst forth:

> "I am Lord of All.
> Hear my voice and weep,
> Oh, miserable creatures of this world.
> Suffer now for all the pain and humiliation
> You have caused me.
> Suffer forever and ever!"

The return of power was glorious. Greater and greater strength filled him.

"I am invincible!"

Idelisia shuddered.

G.W. and Samson paused in a clearing. "What was that?" G.W. said.

The raven troop landed in the nearby trees, nervously shifting along the branches, feathers ruffling unevenly.

"I sense a drastic shift in our world," Fial said, "and it's nothing good. Our enemy to the north must have found new strength. If we don't find the girl soon, I fear for her life." The strain of maintaining his human form was wearing him down, and his voice was unnaturally harsh.

"I know you and your friends agreed we would search for the girl together, but if you're right and our enemy is gathering more power, it changes everything. You and your troop can be more effective searching together, overhead. The cat and I will make our way safely," G.W. said, letting her wand drop into her hand. Magic sparkled along its length.

"Orange Pants has an uncanny sense of smell, in case you doubted this, and together we should be able to make good progress." G.W. smiled gently as Fial shifted back into bird form.

"We'll continue to circle back to you," Fial said as he flew over the towering trees. The raven troop lifted as one and disappeared after their leader.

Samson licked a paw nonchalantly. "Now what, old woman?"

"I was serious, Marmalade Boy. Your sense of smell is extraordinary. Put it to use and let's find that girl."

"Flattery, flattery." He smiled, then lifted his lip. The full *flehming* sounded like *ick-ick-ick*. Sniffing, his whiskers at full attention, Samson prowled ahead of the old wizardess and disappeared into the darkened forest.

His yowl alarmed G.W. and she raced toward the sound. "Samson! What is it? Where are you?"

When she burst into a tiny clearing, the orange cat was crouched close to the ground, the tip of his tail flicking back and forth. His ears and whiskers were laid back against his head. A growl rumbled in his throat.

"I've found something," he said. "It's faint. Like what we found at the cottage, but different. She's been near here, but she's frightened. Or being followed, or maybe tracked." He lifted his head toward G.W. "And something else. I've caught a whiff of the ooze that attacked us back there."

Stifling a gasp, G.W. nodded and held her wand more securely. "Lead on, Orange Prince. We have no time to waste."

The voice in Oelsa's head drowned out her thoughts. She covered her ears and screamed, "Stop it! Stop yelling at me!"

The voice relented. The stillness was more disturbing than the screaming. "Ah, I have your attention, do I?" Smooth, like a snake's skin.

"Father? Please, talk to me. Tell me where you are. I'm trying so hard to find you."

"I'm trying so hard." The voice mocked Oelsa.

Her father had never spoken to her this way. "Why are you talking like this? Don't you want me to find you?"

"Poor girl. So lost in the woods, but so brave." The voice made fun of her and sarcasm laced his words. "Give me what I want, and your dear father will be returned to you, whole and unharmed."

Struggling to wrench her cloak free from a thorn, Oelsa's mind was overwhelmed by the hard, demanding voice. "You aren't my father." She was incensed. "Where have you taken my father? Tell me or I'll never give you what you want." She clutched the yellow stone as she spoke.

"You think you can defy me?" The voice screamed. "FALL TO YOUR KNEES AND GROVEL, WORM!"

The words knocked Oelsa to her knees and pinned her to the ground.

"I WILL HAVE THE KEY!"

"What are you talking about? I don't have any Key."

"Liar! You have what is rightfully mine, and you will bring it to me, or else!"

The "or else" paralyzed Oelsa. Was Father a captive of this madman? "All right. I'll do as you wish." When there was no immediate response, Oelsa pulled herself up, expecting another blow. When nothing happened, she took a few steps and hesitated, unsure where to go or what the violent voice expected. When she touched her yellow stone, seeking comfort and direction, it shocked her. "Ow!"

Insane laughter filled her head. "I was waiting for you to do that, you little fool! You think there's any magic anywhere more powerful than mine?"

The stone burned to the touch. Oelsa dropped it.

"Leave it! Mine is the only voice you need listen to." The hideous laughter grew louder as she stooped to retrieve the yellow stone.

"I said leave it!"

The stone shattered in her hand. Oelsa cried out, "You can't do that!"

But the voice in her head was remorseless. "He's still alive, you know. For a while longer. The faster you move, the more likely you are to find him breathing."

Oelsa let her hat fall. As she reached to pick it up, she snatched the shattered pieces of the yellow stone and pushed the remnants into her pocket.

Propelled against her will, Oelsa stumbled through giant firs thirty feet around, through ferns reaching to her waist, and into clusters of enormous maple-leaf-shaped plants covered with sharp thorns and stinging nettles.

Dread built. The insidious voice raged in her head. "Keep moving if you want to find your father alive."

Unable to resist, Oelsa was guided by the invisible demon. "I will do anything for you, Father. Please hold on just a little longer."

24

ANVYARTACH GLORIED IN HIS NEW STRENGTH. "I'm back! I'm really back, and I'm stronger than ever." To test this, he turned his glance to the pewter goblet at his side and said, "Be gone!" It smoldered briefly and disappeared.

"Oh, my!" the Shadow Lord squealed. "Let me do another!" He set to destroying every piece of tableware near him.

"And what about you, Mangred? Are you still dawdling in that old forest?" He held the glass orb in his sinewy fingers. The orb clouded with gray smoke that sizzled before clearing. "Ah, there you are, Mangred."

In the orb, Anvyartach saw Mangred and his men racing through the trees. "Mangred!" One word, shouted, and his strong, right-hand man stumbled and almost fell.

"Master?" Mangred's voice quavered as he hunched into a protective crouch and cast glances over his shoulders, trying to find the source of the voice.

"Thought you could evade me, did you?"

Mangred tried to make his legs stop wobbling, but intense fear coursed through him. "Where . . . where are you, Master?"

Behind him, the men holding the prisoner's log froze. They could hear the voice, but it seemed to come from nowhere and everywhere at once.

"It doesn't matter where I am, Mangred. Suffice it to say I can now see you and talk with you. You've been falling behind on your job, Mangred. I thought you'd be in my palace some time ago, and yet, I see you are still meandering through the woods, like you're going to some picnic, eh?"

"No, Master! No! We've been moving as quickly as possible, but these trees are . . . confusing. And without a map, it's been, uh, difficult, don't you see?"

"Let me tell you what is difficult," Anvyartach sneered, "Waiting! Waiting for the fulfillment of one simple task. How long do you expect me to wait, Mangred?"

Mangred put his hands to his head and moaned. "Please, Master. Please understand. We're doing our best. I'm sorry you've had to wait, but . . ."

The Master's voice filled Mangred's head. He screamed in pain.

"I am through waiting. Bring me the woodcutter now. And, oh, yes. Find his daughter and bring her as well."

Mangred sat on the ground and searched for the right words. "His daughter? The woodcutter has a daughter?"

"Yes, Mangred, the woodcutter has a daughter, and she's wandering in those same woods as you and your lazy crew. She's coming to Tirvar, and it shouldn't take too much effort on your part to capture her as well."

If Mangred had thought his original task was difficult, he now realized how childishly simple it was compared to finding a girl in this immense and confusing forest. "But, Master, I don't know. I mean, she could be anywhere, couldn't she? This is more complicated than you might think."

"Stop whining, you simpleton."

Trembling, Mangred glanced over his shoulder searching for his Master.

"Hold still, you moron. Since you've been sauntering through the forest, things have changed a bit," the Shadow Lord said. "You may not have known this, but I've been watching you through my glass orb. And recently I've learned the secret of speaking directly to you at the same time."

The glass orb, Mangred thought. *Of course!*

"Stop fidgeting. I'm sending you a special message."

The air around Mangred sizzled, and his matted hair smoked. Clasping his head with both hands, his eyes bulging, Mangred opened his mouth to scream. The next second he fell to the ground, stiffening like the log holding the prisoner. The soldiers stared at their leader in disbelief. "Mangred? M-M-M-Mangred? What's wrong, Mangred?" One of the braver men poked Mangred in the side with his toe.

"He ain't moving!" he said and kneeled beside the fallen leader. "He ain't breathing neither." As he leaned toward his chief, his next words were garbled as Mangred gripped the soldier's throat and squeezed.

"I ain't breathing?" Mangred growled as he pulled himself to a sitting position and released his hold on the unfortunate soldier. "I ain't breathing?!" he roared. "And who said you could get that close to see if I was breathing or not?!" As he rose to his feet, Mangred felt stronger than ever.

"Pick up that log and be quick about it. We have another little errand to do, and you-know-who is tired of waiting!" He cracked Velvet over their heads.

Terrified of this newer, more threatening Mangred, the men heaved the prisoner's log onto their shoulders and hurried onward.

The Shadow Lord had shown Mangred how to find the girl because he could now see the path clearly.

Mangred's thoughts were riddled with unsolved questions, but he knew where he was going. The Master had burned it into his mind. They would find the girl in three days, if they just kept moving.

25

FESTIE, PRINCE OF THE BEETLES, observed his minions from an elevated position in the underground hall. Thousands of beetles gathered over and around the semiconscious Ardreas. Largest of all the beetles, Festie was as big as a fist, and he reveled in the size of their latest conquest. Never had such a colossal victim fallen prey to their traps, and they were all a little dazed by their brazen capture.

"Fes-tie! Fes-tie! Fes-tie!" A thousand tinny voices filled the chamber.

Even though he felt too lethargic to move, Ardreas heard their clamor and knew he had to get moving before their sharp pincers cut him to pieces. His mind knew, but his body wouldn't respond.

The voices chanted louder and called to their prince. "Kill! Kill! Kill!"

"Silence!" cried the Prince of the Beetles. "No one will be killed until I command it!" Festie's voice rang with indisputable authority. The underground room plunged into silence.

Festie looked down on Ardreas and demanded, "What right do

you have to be in our kingdom, intruder? No one enters our realm without our permission!"

Ardreas tried to speak, but the poison slowed the muscles in his tongue. He grunted, but only succeeded in frightening the beetles covering him and they pinched him even harder.

"You refuse to reply?" Festie roared.

As hard as Ardreas struggled to speak, neither his tongue nor his lips would respond.

Festie knew the prisoner couldn't respond and enjoyed tormenting him. "Still refuse to speak? Maybe you need a taste of our special hospitality!"

The room erupted in wild jubilation. In a flash, the beetle horde descended from the ceiling and walls and converged over and around and under Ardreas's body, lifting him a few centimeters above the floor and sprinting with him down another passageway into the darkness.

Light disappeared, the air cooled, and the smell of earth grew stronger. The beetles dashed forward, bumping Ardreas's body against the uneven path.

Hauled away like a sacrificial offering to who-knew-where, Ardreas's thoughts raced. *I need an escape plan. It would be easier if I could see where we're going.*

Unfortunately, each time he tried to turn his head, pincers bit his neck, making it impossible. Rolling his eyes side to side, he perceived he was in a passageway so narrow his head almost grazed the top and his body scraped its sides. Even if he managed to escape, he might not be able to maneuver around the multitude of beetles in the tunnel with him. His thoughts turned to Oelsa. *If she's anywhere near here, I hope she's smart enough to stay away from these monsters.*

The beetles halted abruptly, but Ardreas's body continued its forward motion, sliding downward into a bottomless pit. He tried to scream, but the only sound was a stifled "mmnn-a-r-r-hhh!"

Beetle pincers clacked thunderously as the colossal intruder slid from their backs. "Into the pit!" roared Festie.

Beetle voices filled the air with eerie chanting. "Slice him! Slash him! Crush him to a pulp!" The roar increased. "Bite him! Squeeze him! Make his head explode!"

Chilled by the ferocious words and still unable to use his limbs, Ardreas landed head first with a thud. Dirt ground into his face and mouth. As he lay still, catching his breath, he heard a faint but distinct panting coming from not too far away.

Ardreas's senses warned him something else lived down here at the bottom of this pit. A whiff of feral musk drifted from the corner along with a distinct "Huff!"

That's no beetle. The hair on Ardreas's neck stood up and his eyes widened. Pins and needles pricked his arms and legs, trembling from the accumulated effects of the countless stings he'd endured. His skin was clammy, and the scores of cuts from so many sharp pincers burned. Ardreas's vision was too blurred to see clearly, but his hearing and smell set off warning bells.

He rolled to his side and tried to relax. From the rim of the pit, countless eyes watched him and eager pincers clacked. The din filled the darkness, but when the noise ceased all at once, Ardreas tensed, ready for an attack.

"What are you, you bugger?" he snarled. It sounded like "B-b-b-b-rgh!"

With infinite slowness the massive creature in the corner rose onto its colossal legs. As it moved, the scissoring sounds from hundreds of tiny blades riding over one another filled the dark pit as they were honed and sharpened with each step.

The rasping of the blades increased as the creature advanced step by slow step. Willing his eyes to clear, Ardreas lifted his head and looked into the reddened eyes of a crazed animal, a creature that exuded one thought only: *Hungry!*

As it moved, inexorably, ponderously forward, the walls of the

pit reverberated. As the mountain of blades moved closer and closer, Ardreas couldn't take his eyes off the nightmare bearing down on him. The only place without blades was the small face that held a large mouth with an army of razor-sharp teeth.

Ardreas's brain slipped into primal fear. He scanned the pit for a way to escape, but its smooth sides offered nothing. He estimated that he had fallen at least ten feet, too high for him to leap.

As the creature advanced, Ardreas glimpsed a thin line wrapped around its back leg. Following it with his eye, he saw that it was fastened to a thick nail pounded into the wall. *So he's a prisoner too.*

As the creature drew closer, Ardreas heard the beetles at the rim of the hole chanting: "Eat him, Promelious! Eat him!" The more they chanted, the more agitated the beast became and the faster its quills rasped against each other. Without warning, Promelious lunged at Ardreas, who fell back just out of reach of the creature's gaping mouth. The razor quills swung forward, however, and with every cut, Ardreas's skin burned.

The beetles roared, "Promelious! Promelious!"

Goaded by the noise, the beast snarled and a yellowy mucous dripped from his many rows of teeth. Incensed by his failure to reach his prey, the creature shook its head back and forth and bellowed a raw, frustrated cry.

Thoughts racing madly, Ardreas pressed against the wall hoping to find a crack or a crevice into which he could crawl. No luck. The walls crumbled as he brushed against them, and he clenched a handful of dirt in his fist.

Squealing with indignation, Promelious hurled himself at Ardreas. He might have reached him, but Ardreas threw the dirt into Promelious's eyes. The beast roared and shook his head, quills slicing against each other.

Ardreas scrambled around the pit until he came to the place where Promelious's tether was fastened. He measured its length with his eye, picked it up, and pulled. Hand over hand, Ardreas wrapped the excess rope around the nail, attaching it to the wall. Promelious resisted, but Ardreas dragged him backward, stirring up clouds of dust that blinded Promelious. Howling, the beast lunged, but was yanked back by the shortened tether.

From above, the beetles and their leader, Festie, heard Promelious bellowing, but the clouds of dust blocked their view.

"Get down there!" roared Festie as he kicked at the nearest beetles, dislodging several from where they clung to the lip of the hole.

Scores of beetles tumbled to the floor of the pit near Promelious's mouth and were snatched up. Ardreas flattened himself against the wall as a second shower of hapless beetles plummeted near Promelious and were devoured in a great gulp.

The short tether gave Ardreas room in which to maneuver, but he couldn't stay clear of Promelious forever. His energy was draining away. Ardreas's raspy breathing could be heard in the silence. Promelious sniffed toward the sound.

Maddened by the nearness of this elusive meal, Promelious bellowed and shook his body side to side. Faster and faster the quills scissored together. The beast quivered with rage and strained at his tether. One desperate lunge and the beast would dislodge the nail from the crumbling wall.

Festie peered into the dusty darkness and listened. When he heard Promelious's enraged howl, he suspected the intruder had somehow frustrated the beast's attack.

Without hesitation he cried, "Follow me, beetles!"

Festie scurried through the door into a series of tunnels leading to the prisoners' hole. "Think you can escape punishment so easily, intruder?" Festie sprinted down a dark passage.

Hundreds of enraged beetles poured after him, pincers clacking and their eyes blazing.

26

FESTIE SCUTTLED INTO ANOTHER TUNNEL. "Keep up!" he urged
the mob bustling after him. "Not far now!"

Ardreas felt nauseous and light-headed. He watched Promelious
rock forward and back, tugging hard against the tether. It wouldn't
be long, Ardreas realized, before the beast would reach his meal.
Ardreas stared at the walls of the pit until he saw a long narrow shelf
over Promelious's head.

All I have to do is hoist myself onto the shelf and lay flat, he thought.
Promelious's legs were too short and the quills too cumbersome to
allow it to stand on its hind legs.

Promelious launched himself at Ardreas. The tether held long
enough for Ardreas to scoot past the beast's head, but not before
some of the quills sliced through the skin on his arms and legs. The
burning started at the point of contact and worked inward.

Ardreas leapt at the shelf. His fingers grazed it and slipped off.
Pain shot through his body as Promelious roared near his back.

Ardreas leapt a second time. Adrenaline pumped through him.

His heart pounded. His fingers caught the edge of stone while his feet dangled. Grit on the ledge made it almost impossible to hang on.

Promelious saw his prey dangling within reach and grabbed Ardreas's foot. Ardreas kicked Promelious hard with his other foot, landing several blows against Promelious's unprotected nose. Bellowing, Promelious dropped his prize.

Ardreas hoisted his body up and over the stone ledge. Gasping, he lay on the shelf and willed his muscles to relax. As his breathing slowed and his body eased along the shelf, a beautiful thought filled his mind: *I'm safe.*

Beneath him Promelious bellowed. Hunger gnawed at the beast's guts, and a red fury engulfed him. He threw himself against the wall under the shelf. With each strike, dirt trickled down. Promelious was like a gigantic wrecking ball. Over and over, he threw himself at the wall causing it to reverberate with each wallop. But the shelf held. Ardreas suspected it was part of the granite rock that formed the foundation of this hole.

At the secret back door, Festie felt the vibrations. They were so frequent and so forceful the beetle prince worried the intruder wasn't as helpless as he seemed.

"Hurry! Our appalling pet is in trouble!" Festie didn't want to miss a minute of this spectacle. He reached the back door and paused to let his followers catch up. The opening had silted over from all of Promelious's pummeling. "Start digging!" he ordered the beetles close to him. "When you break through, find the intruder and prod him toward the beast. It will be the best show ever!"

The thought of so much blood and mayhem thrilled Festie. He turned to the hundreds of beetles swarming down the narrow passage and ordered, "Dig!"

27

ANVYARTACH HELD THE GLASS ORB and chanted the words for Far Seeing. As he chanted, he concentrated on finding the FireIce, commanding it to appear before him.

> *Hogenhuder, barla bive.*
> *Calam couthy, argu prive.*
> *Scathefyr!*
> *Swive!*

With each repetition of the spell, green smoke filled the glass, but the FireIce refused to appear. "So, you've taken on a life of your own," Anvyartach guessed. "How marvelous. I created you to increase in strength the more life force you consumed. This is better than I dreamed. You answer only to your need for raw emotion and life energy."

Delighted by the independence of this weapon, Anvyartach stared into the vats of bubbling, tar-like substances. "More FireIce." He said the word with glee. "Soon you'll be powerful enough to subdue all those miserable inhabitants of my world."

As he worked, the Shadow Lord felt his mind gaining more of his old power. Each chanted spell from the old manuscripts strengthened him. "I have returned, Idelisia. There is no forgiveness. You let the First Creators blast me into the ether in a billion pieces, so now you will pay. The Key will make it so!"

Anvyartach's laugh chilled the air as he strolled back to the Great Hall. "I wonder if Mangred has found the girl yet? His failures are so disappointing. Maybe I'll send his friend Uhlak to help him. What a surprise that will be!"

Anvyartach shouted at a quivering slave. "Find my second-in-command and bring him here."

Uhlak was a burly man whose leather armor reached his knees. His head and face were covered with tough barbs of brown hair. His gray eyes held no light. Bending his knee in submission, Uhlak muttered, "I am yours to command."

Hovering over Uhlak, Anvyartach issued his orders. "Take twenty of your best soldiers and find your friend Mangred. Use the new soldiers." After months of trial and development, Anvyartach's newest experimental soldiers were ready. "Mangred has disappointed me. The prisoner should have been before me long ago, along with his daughter. You will complete the task Mangred has failed. These tree soldiers won't fail you."

The tree soldiers were a forest of black spruce before Anvyartach's cruel experiments. He tortured them until their spirits became ghosts of their former majesty and transformed them into semisentient creatures capable of moving tirelessly over the earth. They were Anvyartach's implacable army.

Uhlak nodded and started to back toward the door. He knew these mutated tree soldiers had abnormal strength and were absolutely loyal to their Master. Bowing lower, he said, "As you command, your worship. Where will I find Mangred?"

Anvyartach's blow sent Uhlak head over heels. "Tell you where to find Mangred? Come closer!"

Uhlak crept closer to the towering Master whose eyes glowed as he mumbled words and placed his finger on Uhlak's forehead.

Uhlak screamed and fell to the floor clutching his head.

"See him now, you imbecile?" Anvyartach's scream echoed through the room. "Follow your miserable thoughts and you can't miss him!" His laughter followed Uhlak out of the great hall.

Why me? Uhlak asked himself again and again as he hurried to the tree soldiers' quarters. Failing Anvyartach wasn't an option, but how would he manage these pitiless soldiers? Uhlak's fears multiplied, each darker than the last.

"So satisfying." Anvyartach rubbed his hands together and drew the glass orb toward him. "Where is that girl? She hasn't been listening as much as I'd like. We'll give her a little nudge, an encouragement to keep moving my direction."

He flicked the orb and concentrated on finding the delicate folds of the young girl's mind. In moments he saw into the darkness of Finnis Fews. "So, there you are."

Oelsa flinched and closed her eyes.

"Are you listening to me, girl?" Anvyartach added a pinch to his words that made Oelsa squirm. "Ah, now I have your attention. Soon you will be joined by one of my helpers. He may look scary, but he's under the strictest orders to bring you to me in one piece!"

Oelsa remained silent as he continued to taunt her.

"Are you listening, girl? Nod your head once if you heard me."

She nodded, wordlessly.

"I am watching you. Your cooperation has made your father's *stay* with my men much more pleasant."

When Oelsa remained silent, Anvyartach pinched her sharply. Oelsa doubled over.

"I don't like my words to be ignored, ever. Try it again, and you won't have the strength you need to help your father." His next jab into her mind made Oelsa yelp.

Forcing herself to straighten, Oelsa said, "I will do your bidding." Unfortunately, her thoughts betrayed her true feelings. Anvyartach sent piercing blades of pain into her mind and Oelsa writhed in agony.

"There, there, now. You may have forgotten I can hear *all* your thoughts, but my patience is wearing thin." He twisted the last word into one last stab.

His overwhelming presence vanished as abruptly as it had appeared.

"Oh, Father," Oelsa said, "please know I am trying my best to find you, but this is harder than anything I imagined. Please hold on just a little bit longer."

The fear and rage battling in her heart drained Oelsa. She sank against the trunk of a towering fir tree.

"Do you smell something, Sami boy? I don't like what I think it might be." G.W. held her wand and wove the beginning of a protection spell.

"It's what you think, but my senses aren't detecting anything too threatening. The girl's scent is stronger here. She's been through here recently." Samson rubbed against G.W.'s legs to comfort her and himself.

"That's encouraging. Do you also smell any ravens? I know we told Fial to work with his troop, but I thought he'd swoop back to see us once in awhile."

"What do you expect from a group of birds?" Samson said.

With a hiss of warning, the ground erupted into a foul, black pool, and the FireIce swiftly surrounded the woman and cat, cutting off any escape.

"I thought you said this ooze wasn't close! I call this *very* close!" G.W. and Samson stood back to back. She hurled the first part of the protection spell around them, but the FireIce moved like lightning.

The magical powers bequeathed to her by the long chain of her grandmothers surged, and G.W.'s face radiated generations of intense strength.

Back, creature of the dark.
Shrivel and devour yourself.
Return to the bowels of the earth,
To the evil one who spawned you!

Again and again, G.W. focused the words of magic on the threatening ooze, and for a time it would shrink, only to return and creep closer and closer.

"I'm losing my strength, Orange One. It's stronger than the first time we battled it." G.W.'s voice was raspy, and her arms trembled.

"We can do this," Samson said. He opened his mind further, seeking the deepest sources of his feline power.

Together they slowed the insatiable ooze, but each time they took a new breath, it drove closer. The cat and wizardess called on their deepest reserves of power, hoping to destroy enough of the threat to make an escape, but the force driving the FireIce was ferocious.

"Can't—last—much—longer—Orange—Friend." G.W. knelt on one knee, her wand arm held straight in front of her. The cat's whiskers drooped around his mouth.

Sinking to both knees, G.W.'s voice faltered, and the ruthless ooze leapt at her face, the burning acid scorching her skin. As Samson rose to his full height, summoning his last reserves of magic, he and G.W. were momentarily blinded by a flash of magic. At the same time, they were lifted skyward.

Fial and the ravens had finished their aerial search for Oelsa and were returning to G.W. and Samson. As they drew closer they heard the deadly battle raging beneath them and saw their friends besieged by the FireIce. Fial's magic was so brilliant G.W. and the cat squeezed their eyes shut. It took several moments to realize they were being lifted out of danger. Yowling, his claws extended, Samson was gripped from neck to tail in the talons of Fial's most powerful ravens, including Biab. G.W. was grasped by her clothes and pulled skyward.

Below, the FireIce exploded in a fury of scalding acid, destroying every inch where the cat and woman had almost been incinerated. As suddenly as it had appeared, the FireIce sank beneath the surface of the earth. The stink of death formed a fog too foul to breathe.

When G.W. and Samson were dropped to the ground, they lay still. Gradually their breath returned, and they sat up and laughed.

"I've never been happier to see a bird in my life," Samson drawled. He winced as he accidentally touched one of the many places where talons had held his skin.

"Nor I." G.W.'s voice was hoarse, and her hair was plastered to her head. "And never more grateful for friends. Thank you, Fial, Biab, and all the rest of you beautiful, beautiful birds."

28

FIAL SHIFTED INTO HIS HUMAN FORM and chanted a healing spell. He wove the words into a glowing beam between his hands. At the peak of intensity, he simultaneously clapped and showered the two friends with a cloud of sparkling dust.

The tip of Samson's tail flicked appreciatively. When Biab hopped closer, he wrapped it around her leg. "I thought it might be you."

Biab laughed and hopped up and down. "You're better?" She brushed his ragged side with her wing and chirruped. "Had us a wee bit worried."

Samson stretched gingerly and stared into Biab's black eyes. "Thank you, feathered friend."

She ruffled her neck feathers and *toc-toc-tocked*. "It was a close one, furry fellow." The cat's gratitude touched her.

Samson padded to G.W. and licked her nose. "Come on, old girl. Stop your lollygagging. You've had a lovely rest, but it's time to get moving." He nudged her chin with his head and butted her shoulder harder.

"Come to rouse the dead, have you, Orange Light." G.W. reached for him. "We were almost goners. Let's not do that again." When she laughed, Samson relaxed.

"Can you stand, G.W.?" Fial reached down and took her hand. "We need to keep moving. I don't like how close that evil ooze came to . . ." He couldn't say the words "killing you," but everyone was thinking them.

"You saved our lives again, Raven King," G.W. said. "We're indebted to you and your clan. We will not forget or fail you if ever you need us." She squeezed his hand, leaned close, and spoke a spell for replenishing his spent strength.

Surprised and more than a little pleased, Fial said, "Time is against us, I'm afraid. The trees are agitated like nothing I've felt before. That black ooze was stronger this time, as you no doubt noticed. If it's looking for the girl . . ." He let the thought dangle. No need to say the obvious.

Head down, tail straight up, Samson explored the area. He paused, scratched the ground and sniffed, and moved on. G.W. called, "Any luck, Orange Wonder? Did those birds scare your sniffer right out of you?"

In response, the orange cat shook his head and raced into the underbrush. "I've found something."

Whirling back into raven form, Fial lifted into the air along with the entire troop. G.W. limped after the cat who rushed back to her. "It's faint, but I think the girl has been near here. What's more interesting, though, is the other scent mixed with it—a man's."

G.W. looked surprised. Samson continued. "And then it gets really interesting because his scent is overwhelmed by that of insects. Beetles, I think. Very powerful and it doesn't feel right. The girl was with this man, but the beetle smell is so overwhelming, I can't tell if she still is."

Puzzled by this mingling of scents, G.W. pulled her cloak tighter and hurried along the path after Samson. "Beetles? How could little bugs be upsetting?"

The wizardess called to Samson as he ran ahead, nose to the

ground. "Your nose is never wrong. Keep going. After what we've been through, I'm ready to find anything!"

Overhead, Fial and Biab caught a glimpse of Samson's orange fur as he raced through the trees. Signaling the troop, they chased after him.

Ardreas grimaced where he lay on the shelf, afraid to move lest he fall into the beast's deadly quills. In a maddened frenzy, Promelious roared and threw himself with greater force against the walls, tugging wildly at the tether until, with one great lunge, he pulled the nail free. With no restraint, the beast clattered around the pit snarling, while the rows of teeth in his gaping mouth chomped loudly.

No matter how hard he tried, Ardreas couldn't find a way to escape. He scanned the walls, and as he'd discovered earlier, where the walls weren't packed hard, they could easily collapse, burying anyone trying to dig through them.

A muffled scratching came from somewhere beneath the shelf. Persistent. Regular. *Like a small shovel filling a bucket with sand.*

Scoop. Crunch. Scoop. Crunch.

Grains of dirt pelted Promelious's face just as he launched a new attack. Spellbound, he watched a steady stream of glossy-backed beetles pour from the wall and climb toward the shelf. Promelious rushed forward and gulped a mouthful of squirming insects.

Despite the beast's feasting, swarms of nasty insects reached the shelf and scuttled over Ardreas's legs and up his torso, pinching as they went.

"You'll not take me again!" Ardreas roared as he pushed against the wall and grabbed handfuls. They kept coming. He whirled his arms and whacked them against the wall. He kicked and stomped beetles as they raced over the lip of the ledge. But for every one he dislodged or squashed, ten more swarmed up and over.

"Hurry, G.W.!" Samson yowled his battle cry.

Fial signaled the ravens to follow, and they landed in a flurry of glistening wings around the agitated cat.

"What have you found?" Fial called.

G.W. huffed into the clearing. "Have you discovered the source of the scent, Orange Marvel?"

"It's coming from underground. Not sure you can make your way into that cave, G.W., but something is definitely very wrong in there. Man scent, an overwhelming smell of beetles, and something else, much stronger, wild, angry."

Samson raced into the cave and disappeared. G.W. pushed through the opening and used her wand to light up the darkness. Fial and Biab led the raven troop into the tunnel, flying cautiously just above the cat's back.

Braking just before he tumbled into a deep pit, Samson screamed his warrior cry, warning G.W. to halt. Fial and the ravens swooped over the pit and returned when G.W.'s light revealed the nightmarish scene below them. On a narrow ledge above the floor of the pit, a man covered in hundreds of black beetles was kicking and flailing frantically. In the pit, a maddened beast with sharp, shining blades covering his body howled and threw itself against the walls again and again, causing the walls to tremble and clouds of dirt to fill the air.

With each of the beast's thuds, the shelf with the man fighting the horde of beetles shook. Tunneling beetles whipped into a great frenzy by their leader were weakening the walls around and under it.

Ardreas first was aware of the new presence in the cave when a wing brushed his arm, and then another and another. Ravens swooped over the shelf and swept beetles into the raging beast's mouth.

G.W. caught Samson just as he was about to leap into the pit. "You're no match for that beast. Let me calm it first." She wove her wand in a mesmerizing circle, catching Promelious's eyes. She hummed and gentled his frenzy. When more beetles cascaded onto the floor, he snorted and eagerly gulped them down.

Fial landed on the shelf near the flailing man and was about to send a calming spell when the largest beetle he had ever seen emerged from one of the tunnels above them. Fial shot toward the bug, picked Festie up in his beak, and carried him away.

Ardreas thought he was hallucinating.

When the beetles saw their prince disappear into the mouth of the large black bird, they squeaked in terror and tried to scuttle away through the tunnels. In their haste, many plummeted into Promelious's hungry maw.

Fial flew to the cave's opening, carrying the squirming Festie in his beak.

"Put me down, you mangy bird!" the beetle cried. "Do you know who I am?"

G.W. hurried after Fial with Samson close on her heels. "What on earth is that?" The size of the beetle astounded her. "Has this insect caused the torture of that poor man and beast?" This was no ordinary creature, she realized, and undoubtedly the source of the cruelty inside the cave.

"I'll take him, Fial, but let's put a little spell on him to keep him from scuttling away." Words flew from G.W. and her wand sparked. Festie stopped squirming and lay like a frozen apple.

Shifting into human form, Fial studied the enormous beetle. Samson sniffed it and bared his teeth when he noticed the beetle could still move his eyes. This terrified Festie and pleased the cat tremendously.

"Stop that, Orange Fangs. You're scaring the little bug," G.W. said. She could feel the nastiness emanating from the creature even in his stiffened state. "So, we have some important questions for you, bug, but first we need to know how to get the man and that poor beast out of the pit where you imprisoned them. Perhaps a hidden entrance?"

Festie pretended to be asleep.

"Well, Mr. Fangs," G.W. stroked Samson's back, "he apparently has nothing to tell us. You can have him. You like playing with bugs, don't you, before you eat them? I've watched you bat them about for an hour or more, before chewing off their heads."

"NO!" screamed Festie. His body was still immobile, but he could talk. "NO! I'll tell you everything you want to know. Just don't give me to that cat!"

"So you do have a voice. Where's the back door?" Fial picked up Festie and dangled him in front of Samson's snapping jaws.

"I'll show you, but then you have to let me go. All right?"

Fial gave the beetle to Samson to carry.

Biab flew out of the tunnel. "What are we going to do with the man? He looks like he's been stung a thousand times" She glared at the dangling beetle in Samson's mouth.

"This bug is going to show us the way," Fial said.

Promelious watched the old wizardess enter the pit and listened to her soothing voice. As she neared him, he knelt in front of her. A whispery gargle came from his throat, like a purr, she decided.

"I think he'll come along with no trouble," she said as she coaxed the strange beast toward the exit.

When they had disappeared from view, Samson shook the beetle in his teeth. "You rotten insect. We should leave you here, alone, frozen, and see how you like it." He gave the nasty beetle another shake.

Several ravens stood guard over the man. Biab flew up to him and brushed his face with her wing, waking him. Fial whirled, shifting into human form as magical words poured from him. The air in the dark pit glowed, and the dirt walls shifted into a long slanting incline that ran from the shelf to the floor.

"Gently, Biab. Let him slide down."

With Fial's magic for support, Ardreas made his way out of the terrible pit.

Outside, Ardreas searched the crowd of strangers and demanded, "Where's Oelsa? What have you done with Oelsa?"

29

G.W. GENTLY QUESTIONED ARDREAS. His wounds needed to heal, not to mention his emotional state. "What do you know about Oelsa, and how did you come to be their prisoner?"

Ardreas gave them his name. "I met a girl in the woods and saved her from those WilderOnes."

"Yes, we had our own experience with them."

"We were trying to intercept the men who kidnapped her father," Ardreas continued, "but I was overcome by an overwhelming compulsion to seek my brother."

G.W. interrupted. "You hadn't been thinking about him? Just suddenly had to leave?"

Ardreas nodded and looked down at his feet.

G.W. and Samson exchanged a look. Yet more evidence their enemy was regaining his former strength. "Ardreas, what else can you tell us?"

"Oelsa wanted to go east to find some mythical tower, but I convinced her to take a path that would intercept the kidnappers. At least I hoped it would." His shoulders drooped.

"Do you think she was convinced you were right?"

"She argued at first, but once we were moving, she seemed excited. Like maybe this *was* the right way to find her father. That was all she wanted, to find her father. Me? I think maybe he's no longer alive. The kidnappers have had him a long time. But she was determined."

"Are you strong enough to take us the same way you were taking her?" Fial asked.

Still not comfortable with the raven's shape-shifting, Ardreas hesitated before deciding to trust the tall magician. "I think so. I'm afraid the girl's in big trouble."

Ardreas swayed slightly when he stood, but he looked for the sun and set off into the forest.

"What about the beast?" Samson asked G.W. "The one with the quills a mile long?"

"I think he'll follow me quietly, as long as he has enough to eat."

When G.W. spoke to Promelious, he made the same whispery gargling sound and leaned toward her. When she stepped into the forest, he followed behind like a well-trained but sharp and bristly dog.

"First, we team up with a bunch of birds, and now this, whatever you call it. Who will she pick up next?" Samson grumbled and ran ahead to catch up with Ardreas.

Noticing the cat at his side, Ardreas picked him up. Much to Samson's surprise, Ardreas held him gently and tickled him under his chin. "A fine cat you are," he said and set Samson back on the ground. "Lead the way, old man. Your sniffer is undoubtedly twice as good as my sense of direction."

Mangred and his bedraggled men slogged through Finnis Fews. *Strange*, he thought, *how I can know where we're going, yet getting there remains nearly impossible.* Mangred's mind had absorbed the map Anvyartach had "sent" to him, but every mile forward cost them. The mud had taken a toll on their fading energy, and now this bog.

The tiny island of solid ground on which they rested afforded little room for the men and the heavy oak log. After failing to find a path out of the bog, Mangred realized they would have to retrace their steps.

Mangred peered into the mire and watched as bubbles of decaying vegetable matter rose and popped with a putrid stench. This had been, by far, the worst assignment he'd ever been sent on. He wanted to disappear from Anvyartach's attention just for a minute, slide the log into the mud, and tell the men to take off.

But Anvyartach was all-seeing. Even now, Mangred suspected, he was watching them flounder their way through this impossible mire. No doubt he'd sent others to take over where he'd failed.

He sighed and sank down next to the log. In moments, he fell into an exhausted, troubled sleep.

Astounded by this bit of good luck, Mangred's men watched a few moments to be sure he was really asleep, and, one by one, slipped away from their cruel Master. The bog had a few tufts of solid footing, enough to create the illusion of safety, but within minutes the ragged crew discovered their tragic error. Within ten steps of the solid island where Mangred slept, they sank into the mire. Their deaths came swiftly.

Uhlak jogged ahead of the tree soldiers, managing to stay ten feet in front. When his energy waned, he stopped their march.

"Did I tell you to stop, you dolt?" Anvyartach pierced Uhlak's mind.

"Where—where are you, Master? I just need a little rest." Uhlak cowered as the tree soldiers resumed their march.

"Follow the map, imbecile! Keep moving!"

Uhlak stumbled and ran after the quickly disappearing tree soldiers, shouting, "Wait for me!"

Watching from Tirvar, Anvyartach laughed. "I love my new powers! Every day is better than the last." He snickered with glee. "Those two are going to bring me the prisoner *and* the girl. Won't they love trying to be first to bring them here?" Anvyartach set the glass orb in its stand, rubbed his hands together, and roared.

Mangred awoke with a start. When he called his men, nothing but silence greeted him. Not one of them was on the island. Except for the prisoner's log, he was alone. He calculated his chances of carrying the prisoner's log by himself, even if he could find a way across this swamp, and realized it was impossible. *He's watching,* Mangred thought, *but why didn't he stop the men from leaving?*

The answer hit him—because he has a new plan. *The Master is sending someone to take over where I've failed.* The reality sank in. *And if I want to survive, I have to have a plan now, before he gets here.*

Uhlak staggered through the woodlands with his hardy crew.

These soldiers had been trees, but Anvyartach had used his cruel magic to shape them into human-like soldiers capable of withstanding any trial and remain untouched by emotion or weakness. Their creation was Anvyartach's most recent triumph, and their mindless march through the thick forest proved his power.

Uhlak watched the soldiers marching effortlessly and thought again it was too bad they hadn't been available for Mangred's mission. No doubt they would have moved with mechanical purpose through Finnis Fews, found their quarry, and returned it to the Master weeks ago.

Uhlak snorted as he lurched toward his rival. "Too bad for Mangred."

Thinking and plotting, Mangred lay on the ground of the muddy island. An hour passed with no sign of his adversary, but the longer he waited, the stronger his instincts for self-preservation grew. Adrenaline pumped through his body and his strength and wits revived.

When the first of the tree soldiers appeared, Mangred's thoughts fixed on the only choice he had for escape. Waiting to rise until he saw their leader, he covertly watched as ranks of tree soldiers marched out of the forest and leapt easily onto the island to form a circle around Mangred and the log that held the imprisoned Dahvi.

"Drowning is too good for you."

Mangred focused on the voice. He recognized it and remembered the cold, unsympathetic cretin to whom it belonged.

Uhlak's voice dripped with ridicule. "So high and mighty, Anvyartach's favorite. And here you lie, drowning in the muck. Did your men desert you?"

Mangred squinted up at the towering rival. "Uhlak? You're the last one of the leftovers I expected the Master to pick." He spit at his foot, a gesture that earned him a sharp kick.

Uhlak nodded and strong hands grabbed Mangred and lifted. Their hold was vise-like and Mangred gasped.

"I have a few questions to ask you, maggot." Uhlak's voice had risen to an unbecoming whine. "I like that. Mangred the Maggot!" He laughed like a crazed dog.

Timing had to be just right, Mangred realized. Intentionally offending the pompous Uhlak, he drawled, "What made the Master choose you? Must have been desperate. Last I knew you were a mere footslogger, grateful for any slops thrown down by my friends."

Uhlak punched Mangred.

Forcing a smile for his enemy, Mangred laughed. "You've always settled things with your fists. Not too bright, our Uhlak." Mangred sneered as he twisted against the tree soldiers' grips.

Uhlak's face flamed with anger.

"I suppose he told you this was simple enough even for a moron like you," Mangred said. Uhlak lunged for his hated adversary. The tree soldiers, caught by surprise, momentarily eased their grip on Mangred. He wrenched himself out of their grasp, tackled Uhlak, and knocked him into the slippery mud. Rolling in the muck, no matter how Uhlak flailed, Mangred was stronger.

As they rolled closer to the edge of the island, Mangred shifted his weight, kneed Uhlak in the stomach, clamped his legs around his chest and squeezed. Uhlak squirmed to free himself, but Mangred pushed his face into the slime. "Order them to back off or you'll die." Mangred inched them farther into the murky bog.

Uhlak jerked up his head and saw madness in Mangred's eyes. "Stand back!" he screamed at the tree soldiers. He gasped for air, terrified that Mangred's next move would be to submerge his head in the slimy water.

When the tree soldiers obeyed, Mangred loosened his grip slightly. Uhlak's plea for help was a garbled, "A-a-a-r-r-g-h!"

Mangred tightened his grip and squeezed. He leaned over and whispered into Uhlak's ear. "Struggle all you wish. I can hold on to you forever, or until all your ribs crack and your lungs explode."

Uhlak gasped harder as the pressure increased. "Let—me—go," he wheezed. "I'll—do—what—ever—"

"Anything?" Mangred said.

Gasping for breath, Uhlak pushed against Mangred's grip but couldn't move. His face was an inch from the swamp water.

"Tell your men they must never attack me under any circumstance."

Uhlak squeaked the required command. The tree soldiers dropped their arms and froze in place. Mangred released Uhlak who rolled on his side and choked out dirty water.

Before Uhlak recovered, Mangred pushed him onto his back and pressed his knee down hard on his throat, groping in the mud for Velvet. When his fingers wrapped around the familiar handle of his whip, Mangred held it near Uhlak's face. "I'll release you, Uhlak, on one condition."

Uhlak's eyes bulged and his tongue protruded.

"I'm number one," Mangred said. "The tree soldiers take orders from me and only from me. Agreed?"

Uhlak, losing consciousness, managed a nod. As he went limp, Mangred removed his knee. "Much better." Mangred straightened and his own ragged breathing calmed.

The tree soldiers remained motionless around Mangred and the limp Uhlak. "Don't worry. He's still alive. Just less eager to give commands."

As the adrenaline drained from his body, Mangred's legs buckled and he dropped into the mud. "That was a close call," he mumbled as he looked at the force Uhlak had brought to subdue him. Mangred lifted his head and howled. "My luck is back!"

Anvyartach watched the confrontation. "Well, well, well. My man Mangred has a few tricks of his own. He'd better use the gift I've sent with that fool, Uhlak, better than he did." He glared into the glass orb. "Find the girl and bring her to me. No more fooling around."

30

THE RAGTAG GROUP STRUGGLED through Finnis Fews while the ravens explored from above, seeking clues to the girl's disappearance. Promelious trotted behind G.W., his spikes rustling.

After a few hours following a faint trail, Ardreas whistled for Samson. "Hey, cat! Give your nose a rest. Looks like we're going to have some interesting weather."

At the sound of the whistle, G.W. chuckled. "Why didn't I ever think to do that?"

Samson raced back, radiating displeasure. His ears were laid flat to his head, and his fangs were bared. His fur stood up on his back and a low growl rumbled through his body. "Whoa, buddy . . ." Ardreas cut his words short when Samson's growl turned to hissing. "OK! OK!" Ardreas put his hands up to ward off the cat.

"I believe he objects to being whistled at," G.W. said. "And maybe to being called 'buddy.' He's a rather proud feline. Comes from an auspicious line of warriors. Perhaps you didn't know." She spoke to Ardreas then stared at Samson and mouthed, "Be good."

Samson flicked his tail and sauntered away, lightly bumping G.W.'s leg.

"You'd almost think he understood your words, G.W."

"He does." With a flick of her wand, G.W. touched Ardreas's forehead, whispered a few words, and waited for the man's gaping mouth to close. "Now you'll be able to understand Samson and the ravens, too."

Ardreas stared, unblinking, until G.W. touched his arm. "It's a little disconcerting the first time you hear animals speak. You'll get used to it." She smiled and lifted her gaze. "Look at that sky."

Heavy clouds scudded from the west of Finnis Fews. The temperature dropped, and G.W. pulled her old, brown cloak more tightly around her. The wind picked up, thunder rolled, and flashes of lightning split the air. Promelious showed no sign of worry as he snuffled along the trail looking for something to eat.

"Samson, come ride on my shoulder," G.W. said. "Keep me warm."

The orange cat, however, crouched and sniffed the air. His fur rose along his back again, and his tail twitched. More lightning split the darkened sky and the bang of thunder exploded almost overhead. The sudden deluge slashed at the three of them as they rushed to find a protected place. Another flash of lightning landed in the same spot where they had stood seconds before. The air reeked of ozone, and Samson's fur crackled with static. "That felt personal."

Fial returned with no warning as though he'd been blown there by the ferocious wind. He clung to the elm branch and called to G.W. The wind carried his words away. Standing near the elm, G.W. raised her head and spread her arms wide. Her wand quivered in her left hand as her lips moved without stopping.

Fial strained to hear the chant that rippled with a singsong rhythm, repeating and repeating, until a gray-green light wrapped around the wizardess. The light thickened into walls impervious to the heavy rain. She relaxed for a moment and called Samson to join her. The bedraggled cat slunk forward and slipped through the glowing walls.

Fial heard an order from G.W.'s mind. "Join us." The next moment he was whisked into the shelter whose walls shimmered with a green light. The hum of the woman's voice rolled around him. Disoriented, Fial felt as though he were tumbling headfirst into a bottomless pit. Vertigo threatened to tip him into a nauseous spin, but G.W.'s will snapped him out of the whirling spell.

"That was close. Where's Ardreas?" G.W.'s voice lifted again in the same singsong manner, and in another minute Ardreas practically flew into the shelter the wizardess had created.

"Some trick, G.W.," Fial said. "Wish the others could find their way inside here."

G.W.'s chant rose again, whirring like a metal wheel caught by the wind. The walls shifted and shimmered, growing translucent as they stretched. In another moment, they were surrounded by all the ravens, shivering and setting up a racket of excited chatter.

"Where did you learn to do that?"

G.W. smiled.

The ravens filled the space with their *Cr-r-ruck, cr-r-ruck, cr-r-rucks*.

G.W. lifted her voice over the ruckus. "We're safe for the time being." She pointed to the shimmering green walls. "But the spell won't last until morning, especially if it's still storming." The sounds coming through the walls suggested the storm's rage was unlikely to end any time soon.

No one noticed the absence of the scissory beast.

"Do I smell singed bird feathers?" growled Samson as he stepped from behind G.W.'s legs. "Yow! Whole bunches of bird feathers." He shook himself from head to tail and water flew from his wet fur.

Fial's voice rose above the din. "We need to thank our friend G.W. for providing us shelter."

The birds lowered their wings and turned their backs on the wet cat who proceeded to wash every inch of his body with meticulous care.

Fial said, "Before G.W. whisked me to safety, I saw, not far away, what looks like an opening under a rocky overhang."

"How far?" Biab asked.

Before Fial could respond, G.W. said, "Doesn't matter. Let's go. Flying in the storm can be dangerous, but I'll provide some protection, enough to break the brunt of the wind and deflect some of the rain."

No one wanted to face the storm again, but when Fial passed among them, soothing their feathers, and complimenting them on their courage, they all agreed to follow his lead.

As they stepped through the green glowing walls of their shelter, rain lashed them and wind buffeted their bodies. Fial lifted into the air determined to find the rocky shelter. The air filled with the troop of ravens who managed to follow Fial's lead.

The translucent walls thinned around them as G.W. and Samson leaned into the storm with Ardreas close behind. In moments, Samson's coat was soaked, and he had to fight for each step. Mumbling the words of the spell continuously, G.W. scooped him up and set him on her shoulder as they fought their way after the birds.

The storm's fury built and the rain turned to icy sleet. Wet to the skin, Samson burrowed into the backpack but kept his head poked out to watch their progress. Hair streaming with water, Ardreas dashed it away. G.W.'s water-logged cloak hung heavily on her shoulders.

The storm flashed and raged. G.W. felt icy rivulets pour down her neck. Samson was stiff with cold. Ardreas pulled him out of the backpack and held him under his arm hoping to share some of his body heat.

"Here," G.W. said through chattering teeth. "Under here." She crawled under the protective boughs of a low-growing evergreen. They huddled together for warmth, while the worst of the storm continued to rage around them.

"Can you smell anything in this maelstrom, Orange Ice?" G.W.'s nickname was intended to make Samson laugh.

Coughing from deep in his chest, Samson shook and clamped his teeth together.

"I've got him. He's shaking pretty hard." Ardreas cradled the orange cat closer to his chest. G.W. noticed the man was also shaking, and his lips were light blue.

"Good man, Ardreas. He's a heavy bundle of fur, especially when he's soaked, but he'll appreciate your warmth." She dug out the blanket from the backpack, still partially dry, and draped it around the man's shoulders. Ardreas lifted one arm and tilted his head to indicate she should join them, a gesture that touched G.W. Hours passed and the three huddled under the tree's limbs. Gradually, one by one, they drifted into a cold and miserable sleep.

Before the earliest hint of dawn, the worst of the storm passed. The thunder stopped rumbling and the lightning disappeared, but a steady, cold rain continued.

Roused from a troubled dream, G.W. gently lifted Ardreas's arm from her shoulders. "Rain before seven, clear by eleven," she hummed to herself. "Or at least that's what my grandmother always said. Of course, this isn't like any storm she ever saw."

Ardreas awoke, almost dropping Samson from his stiff arms where he'd managed to cradle the cat throughout the night. "So stiff," he whispered as he tried to stretch his arms and legs.

"Here, I'll take him." G.W. lifted Samson into her arms. "Oh, my. He's burning up, isn't he? We've got to get something warm inside him."

Ardreas felt around in his pockets until he pulled out a flat, metal bottle. "It's the last of my brother's cider. I was saving it for a rainy day." Tipping it toward Samson's mouth, Ardreas realized the cat wouldn't know to open up, so he dropped a little onto the tail of his shirt and squeezed it around Samson's teeth. The cat opened his mouth, and Ardreas tipped several more drops of cider down his throat. "It's gone a bit hard, but maybe it'll warm his belly."

G.W. said, "He needs rest and food, and some of my special elixir.

You're not the only one with good medicine, Ardreas." She rummaged in her pack and pulled out an amber bottle with opaque sides. She pulled out the stopper and dropped a little into Samson's mouth.

"You're next, young man," she said, and ordered Ardreas to take a swallow.

"But there won't be enough for you."

Her face was so stern he followed her directions. In moments, his skin suffused with color and he coughed slightly. "What's in that stuff? It's great."

G.W. took a few drops for herself and felt her insides warming. "That's better. Thanks to your kindness, Ardreas, Fuzzy Pants is going to make it." She rubbed his head and under his chin and was relieved to feel a tiny purr in his throat. "Ready?"

Ardreas crawled from under the tree's low limbs and reached his hand to G.W. Wrapped in the wool blanket, Samson rode in the backpack.

Hungry, cold, and wet clothing against their skin, they set off with Ardreas in the lead, guessing at the right direction. G.W. mumbled as she walked, and her wand sparked little stars. When she touched it to the next towering fir, she paused to listen. "Stay to the right, Ardreas. Careful you don't slip on those muddy leaves."

Their feet were soaked as well, and they managed to stay upright only by grasping wet tree limbs that spilled more water over them. Miserable, they pushed on, guided by luck, Ardreas's uneven sense of direction, and G.W.'s deft magic that spoke to the drooping trees.

The trees whispered into G.W.'s mind: *This way. This way. Hurry. A treacherous evil stalks her, and a much worse force pulls her into danger.*

Promelious didn't find the clearing where G.W. had created the green glowing shelter until after they were gone. In the midst of lightning flashes and strong winds and thunder rolls, he tried to find the first person to show him kindness. Nothing but her scent was left, and he wailed mournfully. He wanted her warm, comforting presence.

Disappointed, Promelious drew his bladed armor tight around him, his protection against the elements and solution for keeping warm through the night.

In the morning, still yearning for the comfort of the wizardess, Promelious bawled his longing to the trees and set out to find her. Although her scent was light, the creature's highly sensitive nose, twice as sensitive as any cat's, allowed him to track the object of his love.

31

THE STORM LASHED AGAINST OELSA. She leaned into the cold wind and pounding sleet. *Father, I'm coming. Please hold on just a little longer.* Mysteriously, the voice that had compelled her forward remained silent. The storm drenched her cloak and before long she could no longer feel her feet or her hands. Desolate and alone, Oelsa's determination weakened. *Why did I abandon Ardreas or the ravens? All they wanted was to help me.*

Hunching her shoulders, Oelsa doggedly kept moving until a darker thought wormed into her mind. *What made me think I'd ever find you, Father? If ever you're going to speak to me again, now would be a good time.*

Disconsolate when no voice responded, Oelsa slogged along the muddy path. The colder and wetter she became, the more miserable she grew, but she persisted.

When faint words broke into her mind, Oelsa was unprepared to fully comprehend them. "... find ... Key! You know where ... must have it!"

"Father? Is that really you?"

Anvyartach stared into the glass orb and watched the smoky vapor swirl. While his magic was stronger each day, the concentration needed to manifest the Far Speaking took more energy than he had. Sending his voice out to Mangred and Uhlak had exhausted him.

As he held the orb in his lap, his thoughts ranged from Tirvar into the deep forest. Memory after memory marched through his mind, each carrying fresh reminders of all the humiliations from the First Time. "I haven't forgotten anything, Idelisia. It's my turn to make you suffer. And you *will suffer.*"

Vengeance lacerated his mind as he gripped the orb. "I know all about your plan to thwart me. I have the woodcutter and he knows about the Key. If he refuses to tell me its secret, his daughter will pay the price of his silence. When they are brought before me, neither one will be able to resist."

Moving like an automaton, Oelsa wrapped her arms around herself, holding her sodden cloak close to her body. The cold bore into her. "That was you, wasn't it, Father? I don't understand what you meant about the Key. Speak, so I can understand."

But no voice reached into her mind. Oelsa's courage ebbed still further. She rested against a rock and held her head in her hands. "You're speaking in riddles. I know nothing about a Key, or where it is. You have to be clearer."

Anvyartach wrestled with his frustration. He rubbed the surface of the glass orb and spoke the magic words that would allow him to see into the depths of Finnis Fews and find the girl. His insistent badgering had no success. "I'm speaking to you, girl! You can't ignore me!" His irritation grew. "I had full contact with that brat an hour ago. She was moving closer to me, but now she's disappeared. Answer me!"

Anvyartach pounded his fists against the cold throne's arms. Too restless to wait, he shifted his attention. "Mangred! I'm watching you!" he shouted. "Are you still following the path I showed you? You don't look like you've made much progress since besting that useless Uhlak! I want that woodcutter and his wretched daughter NOW!"

"If I could just sleep a moment . . ." Oelsa's teeth were chattering and her body was heavy and unresponsive. Willing herself to stand, she steadied her hand against the rock. "Talk to me, Father. I'm not giving up until I find you."

Anvyartach saw something in the orb that resembled a small person, yet the features were so indistinct, he wasn't sure. "Is that you, that sodden mess that looks like a wet animal? Where is the Key, girl? Don't you dare disappear before you give me the secret."

When the girl did not respond, all the anger that had been brewing suddenly burst. Raising the orb above his head, Anvyartach shouted, "I command you to speak to me, girl. BRING ME THE KEY!"

32

THE STORM HAD BEEN TOO POWERFUL for the ravens to stay close to G.W. and Samson. They were blown over a wide expanse of the woods and separated. Biab's strength allowed her to keep track of Fial and several of the younger ravens, and they eventually landed in the branches of a tall fir. Fial tried to set off in search of his crew, but Biab's voice of reason pulled him back. "They're scattered who knows where. In this darkness, you'll never see them. You'll end up dashed against some tree trunk, and what good would that be to anyone?"

Not the words he wanted to hear, but his own exhaustion kept him hunched on the tree branch. When the storm eased and the earliest hint of light allowed, Biab rustled her soaked feathers. "Let's move. I need to work up some heat."

Relief flooded the troop when Biab, Fial, and the youngsters at last found them. As they straggled into camp, Biab teased, "You're the sorriest mass of feathers I've ever seen."

The troop's joyful *krk-krk-krks* filled the air.

"Any sight of G.W. and that cat?" Fial asked. "Hard to say where they were blown in that storm. Anyone strong enough to look for them?"

Brand'oo volunteered immediately, but Biab stepped in front of him. "I'll find the wizardess and her cat. I've a few things to say to that fur ball."

When Fial nodded his approval, Brand'oo ruffled his feathers in displeasure. He didn't like being left out.

Fial noticed his friend's reaction and added, "Biab does have a certain connection with that cat, and besides, she has the best eyesight of us all. We'll split up and continue searching. Brand'oo, I need you to lead the first group. Who knows, you might even find the girl."

Exhausted from the pounding they'd taken from the storm, none of the ravens felt ready for more searching, but if Fial asked, they would go. Brand'oo selected a dozen older ravens and set off toward the north. Biab lifted off shortly afterward, circled overhead, and flew west.

"Come on," Fial encouraged the remaining ravens. "We'll head east, make a long swoop, and return. Anyone unable to fly more than a mile, however, should stay here. Rest."

Several were too tired to keep their eyes open, willingly settled into the welcoming branches, and dropped into deep sleep. When a dark pool formed at the base of their pine tree, their exhaustion made them easy prey. Launching itself upward, the FireIce consumed the trunk in seconds, which caused the tree to crash with all the ravens caught in its branches. The rapacious FireIce raced over the fallen tree and devoured the struggling ravens.

None escaped.

The FireIce's craving for life energy was insatiable. Where once had been a living tree and a score of ravens, nothing remained but a reeking black hole. The FireIce sank back into the earth.

Disappointed she hadn't found the cat or the humans, Biab flew back the way she came. As she drew close to where she was certain she had left the troop, a cold dread washed over her. Where the tree had stood, only a gaping hole with the smell of death remained.

Horrified Biab screamed, "No! Not the youngsters and Brand'oo! NOT FIAL!"

The morning when the black ooze had attacked their troop and the girl had disappeared flashed through Biab's mind. This had to be the same ooze Fial had barely been able to control. Why hadn't she expected such a weapon to follow and attack again?

Biab leapt into the air and flew blindly away. *I killed them!* echoed in her head.

None of the ravens found their missing friends. Their disappointment deepened the moment they neared the pine where they'd left the remainder of their troop. Only the stinking residue greeted them.

The enormity of these deaths crushed Fial. Unable to speak the grief he felt, he flew into the darkened forest, the distraught troop close behind. As he flew, dread filled Fial's mind. *Why didn't I see this coming? Where is Biab?*

Mangred ordered the tree soldiers to pick up the prisoner's log and march from the swampy island. Mangred grinned maliciously. "Get a move on, Uhlak!" When Uhlak didn't move, Mangred cracked his whip.

Cringing from Velvet's licks, Uhlak dodged the second snap of the whip. A disc slipped from Uhlak's cloak pocket and landed next to Mangred's foot.

"What's this?" Mangred snatched it up. "You sneaky dog! You have more guts than I'd have thought possible. You stole one of Anvyartach's favorite toys! The Hunt Disc!" Mangred howled with laughter as he gave Uhlak another shove. "Oh, you're going to pay for this!"

Pushed beyond his endurance and feeling more terrified with every taunt, Uhlak fainted.

"Pick him up!" Mangred ordered the nearest tree soldier. "Don't damage him, though. I want him in one piece when we return to the Shadow Lord. I want to watch what happens!" What a delightful and predictable ending for Uhlak.

Mangred had heard stories about the Hunt Disc and its special powers for revealing directions, but he'd never used it. *When Uhlak regains his senses,* he thought, *I'll demand a demonstration. With this device, finding the girl and returning to Tirvar with both prisoners is a snap.*

He set the tree soldiers on a brisk march through the forest. Things had taken a definite turn for the better. Maybe he'd survive this assignment after all, especially when he was the one to present Anvyartach with the prizes.

A few hours later, when the storm hit, Mangred was unprepared. As the pelting rain turned to sleet, he had to push to stay ahead of the inexhaustible tree soldiers. No matter how strong the wind, the relentless soldiers continued to march at the same steady speed.

"Slow down," Mangred croaked, but his words were blown away. Clawing his way forward, he turned toward one of the front soldiers and shouted. "Slow down!" Their pace slackened slightly.

The cold rain awakened Uhlak, but he pretended to be unconscious. Being carried through this miserable storm was much easier than walking. When Mangred caught sight of his shifty glances, he shouted to the tree soldier, "Halt! Put him down!"

Mangred grabbed Uhlak by the shoulder. "Tell me how to work the Hunt Disc! Finding the girl in this storm is next to impossible unless we use it!" He shook Uhlak and jammed the Hunt Disc in his face.

This was a break Uhlak hadn't expected. "Ah hah! So I have some use after all. What's it worth to you?"

The two glared at each other as the storm intensified. "Show me where to find the girl," Mangred said.

"Girl?" Uhlak was puzzled. "The Master said nothing about a girl."

"The plan has changed. We're picking up a girl, but this storm is making it impossible to see the path."

Uhlak shouted over the driving sleet. "The Disc needs a specific person or place."

"It's a girl, in the woods, making her way toward us . . . from somewhere!"

"Describe the girl," Uhlak said.

The tree soldiers were frozen in place, holding the prisoner's log, waiting to resume their mission. As the sleet lashed against the two henchmen, they huddled closer together. "We need shelter!" Uhlak shouted. "Can't see anything."

Mangred grabbed him and shook him. "We can't stop! The prisoner is too far gone. If we wait, he'll not make it to the Master alive and that isn't going to happen on my watch! Show me how to use the Hunt Disc, now!"

Pulling free of Mangred, Uhlak darted in among the tree soldiers and wrapped himself around the largest one. "Carry me," he whispered. The tree soldier bent stiffly, lifted the man to his middle section, and waited.

"March!" Uhlak ordered.

The tree soldier hesitated, unsure which man to obey.

"March!" Uhlak ordered again, his voice echoing familiarly to the tree soldier who lifted one foot and shuffled forward. "Faster!" Uhlak commanded. When the tree soldier complied, Uhlak giggled insanely and shouted to Mangred, "Try and catch me!"

Exasperated, Mangred watched his enemy, Uhlak, disappear into the heavy sleet. "After him!" Mangred screamed, and the tree soldiers resumed their mindless march.

33

"I'LL KILL BOTH OF YOU!" Anvyartach watched Uhlak escape from Mangred. "I have to admit, Uhlak, you surprise me. You'll regret stealing the Hunt Disc, but you've outsmarted Mangred for the time being. Not bad!"

Anvyartach laughed as he worked the glass orb and spoke the spell for Far Speaking. "Mangred! What are you playing at? Forget Uhlak and get back to your task."

Racing through the howling wind and the biting sleet, Mangred was focused on catching Uhlak and not listening to his Master.

"Mangred!"

Mangred stumbled. "What is it, Master?"

"Find the girl and forget Uhlak! You have the Hunt Disc. Use it!"

The command was so forceful Mangred grabbed his head and yelled, "I don't know how to use it, Master! You never showed me!"

A painful jab shot into Mangred's forehead.

"Listen, you fat-headed moron. You only have the Disc because of that brainless Uhlak. I'll send the directions. Once!"

Mangred watched the tree soldiers march out of sight. "Wait!" The storm whisked his voice away.

As the instructions for using the Hunt Disc pounded into him, Mangred fell. Bright lights flashed across his eyes as the message sank into his brain.

Before Mangred could rise, Anvyartach demanded, "Where's the prisoner?! Have you lost him too?"

Lurching to his feet, Mangred plunged after the tree soldiers. They trampled the undergrowth, but their path was erratic. "Can't lose the prisoner. Can't lose the prisoner," he repeated as he ran.

The rain beat into Mangred. As long as he kept moving, he could stay warm, but any slowdown made him shiver uncontrollably. The wind howled, and he picked himself up one more time and darted down the path they had taken. When he still couldn't see them, indecision plagued him. "Who should I search for first—the girl or the tree soldiers with the prisoner?"

Mangred knew the prisoner's life was ebbing away, and the sooner he was delivered to the Master, the better. But the Master also commanded him to bring the daughter, and who knew where she might be wandering in these woods?

Taking a terrific risk, Mangred called out, "Master! You have the power to speak to the tree soldiers. Command them to halt!"

Waiting for the jolt of pain following such an impertinent demand, Mangred cowered. Sleet dripped down his face and under his vest.

"Good idea, Mangred," the voice oozed into his mind. "They will be waiting for you."

Mangred waited for another blow from the Shadow Lord. When nothing happened, he leaned against an ancient hemlock and hauled out the Hunt Disc. He stared at its surface and blanched. The Shadow Lord had sent instructions, but which part should he move first? The blue ring with numbers? The red one with unfamiliar symbols? The indecipherable words written in gold on the glossy black ring?

Moving one ring against another, Mangred winced when a sharp edge bit his fingers. He nearly dropped the disc when it shocked him. Mangred's hand hovered over the disc. *Calm yourself,* he thought. He tentatively touched the symbols and when nothing shocked him, he relaxed enough for the instructions to appear. Move the red ring two notches clockwise. Now the blue ring with numbers. He tapped it lightly, and when nothing bit his fingers, he moved the ring counterclockwise until it refused to move further. Before he could tackle the black ring with the golden words, it twirled with lightning speed around the two circles, stopping so one word showed through the center of the disc: CONCENTRATE.

Focusing hard, Mangred pictured the tree soldiers as he'd last seen them. The disc buzzed, and the third ring flashed around the disc, stopped, and ordered: This way! When Mangred stepped in the correct direction, the disc whirred and filled him with comforting warmth. Barely able to believe his luck, Mangred reeled down the faint path. *If I ever find you, Uhlak, I don't know whether I'll cuff you for running away or give you a bear hug for bringing me this amazing device.*

Squirming out of the snug blanket, Samson coughed when he leaned over G.W.'s shoulder. "Chilly! What happened to the sweet, balmy days of fall?"

"Oh, ho! You've finally awakened from your nap, have you, Orange Love?" G.W.'s voice, thin with cold, warmed Samson's heart. He pulled himself completely from the pack and leapt to the ground.

"Thank you for saving my furry hide." He sniffed the wet ground and shook his paws. "This drizzle has made the girl's scent almost imperceptible. But I'm catching a different scent, very strong. Birds!" He choked as he said the last word.

Ardreas grabbed for the cat who slipped easily from his grasp and darted away. "Hey, Lightning! You didn't shrink away when you were freezing." He glanced at G.W. "Does he really know where to go?"

Before G.W. could respond, Samson dashed back, bumped hard into Ardreas's legs, and tore off again. "Follow me, big oaf, if you can keep up!"

Laughing, Ardreas and G.W. set off into the woods, trying to keep up with the streak of orange racing ahead of them. G.W.'s wand emitted sparks to light their path. When she touched the old cedar leaning across their path, she heard its message: *Hurry!*

The storm's fury abated and the cold deepened. Fial called for a break from their search for the girl. The quivering ravens dropped into the branches of the ash and cleaned their feathers.

Hunched on the ground, Fial hopped in a tight circle. Black thoughts plagued him.

"Leave me alone, Brand'oo."

Brand'oo halted, but his words were strong. "You could do nothing to prevent that wicked attack. Even if we had known that foul ooze was following us, I don't believe we could have stopped it. You remember how quickly it moves. We barely managed to haul G.W. and that cat out of its maw. Blaming yourself gets us nowhere."

Head lowered, Fial said, "But I could have tried. Now there's no way to bring those friends back!" The mournful words caught in his throat.

"We need your leadership more than ever, Fial. As bad as this is, we have to keep going. The girl's life is threatened, and we have to find G.W., that cat, and the tree man, Ardreas, before this wretched weather gets worse." He didn't add, ". . . before they're destroyed by the growing evil in the north."

"You're right, Brand'oo, but I have to know what's happened to Biab. Do you think she was there and . . ." The words choked off as he tried to voice his worst fear.

"No way to know. She's strong. If she can, she'll find us. That's all we can hope for."

Fial closed his eyes, shook himself, and stood tall. "Let's get this raggedy crew back in the air. There's no time to waste, as you so eloquently pointed out." He touched his wing to Brand'oo's shoulder, then lifted into the air and called the troop: *Cark! Cark! Cark!*

When the tree soldiers abruptly halted, the prisoner's log swung forward a few inches then swung back into place. The motion stirred the prisoner to consciousness. Dahvi's senses were fading. Sight had faded first, then taste. Lingering smells came and went, but Dahvi was most aware of the pervasive smell of tree sap. Sounds drifted in and out of his prison—voices as well as a sharp snap, like the sound of a whip. But his mind was so disoriented that he had trouble differentiating real sounds from imaginary ones.

"Am I talking out loud, or are the words simply rolling around my mind?" He couldn't decide. "I should have told Oelsa years ago about her gift. But she was just a child, and the danger was so unimaginable. I should have told you of the Key, Oelsa, before it was too late."

As his imprisonment lengthened, Dahvi's inner sense of self faded, as did his ability to form thoughts. "Oelsa . . ." He tried to mouth the word but his lips and tongue no longer responded.

"O-o-e-l-l-s-s-s-s-s-a-a . . ." The sound still resonated in his heart. "You—are—the—*KEY!*"

"NO-NO-NO-NO! YOU CAN'T DIE! I must have your SECRETS!" Anvyartach shook with impotent fury.

The voice was so faint Oelsa wasn't sure at first if she'd actually heard anything. "Father?" Oelsa waited. Shivering hard, she pulled her soggy cloak around her.

"Your voice is so low, Father. I can barely hear you." The words stuck in her throat as understanding flooded into her. "NO! Father! Don't leave me!" Oelsa begged, "Don't die! Please, Father! I need you!"

She had failed to save her father. "I'm sorry. I'm so sorry!" The new question buzzed in her mind. "What did you mean 'I am the Key'?"

34

DEEP, INEXHAUSTIBLE CRAVINGS propelled the FireIce through Finnis Fews, its one coherent desire to devour *emotions! Energy! ALL LIFE!*

The wind howled, bending the treetops to the ground. Mangred stumbled onward, his body bent, his teeth chattering, and his hands numb. "Must keep going," he chanted as he raced on, directed by the Hunt Disc.

"Maybe Master didn't stop the tree soldiers. That would be just like him. I should have overtaken them by now."

"YOU BLITHERING IDIOT! HE'S DEAD!"

The shock of Anvyartach's rage in his head paralyzed Mangred. He doubled over with pain. "Who are you talking about?" But Mangred knew. The prisoner was dead.

"FIND THE GIRL! SHE HAS THE SECRET KEY! FIND HER BEFORE SOMETHING HAPPENS TO HER, TOO!"

The pain stopped as suddenly as it started. Pulling himself to his feet, Mangred ran in the direction the Hunt Disc had shown him.

"If I ever complain again about being too hot, slap me." Ardreas shivered. The frigid wind blew right through him.

G.W. huddled deeper into her cloak and nodded. Her shoes were soggy and her feet icy. She clamped her mouth shut to keep her teeth from chattering. "We must keep moving."

"Of course," Ardreas said confidently, but the length of his strides had shortened in the last hour. "That cat does know where he's taking us, doesn't he?"

"I've never known his nose to fail."

Samson raced into view and yowled. "It's happened again. You'd better see this for yourself."

Ardreas and G.W. stopped at the edge of the stinking hole where the FireIce had attacked and consumed the ravens. The foul reek of death overwhelmed them. "Oh, no," groaned G.W.

"There's a powerful scent of raven," Samson said.

This was Ardreas's first contact with the FireIce and the stench hit hard. "What is that? It's not natural, is it?" He swallowed hard to keep from throwing up.

"We've battled it twice, barely escaping each time," G.W. said. "And we've heard stories of other attacks, namely against Oelsa. Now this. How I hope it didn't destroy all those amazing ravens." Her eyes welled with tears as she imagined such a loss.

A subdued G.W. stepped away from the stinking residue. "We need to keep searching for the girl. It's possible most of the ravens escaped."

Ardreas stood back from the crater. His shoulders slumped. He was more miserable than any time he could remember. The attack of the beetles and the fight with Promelious paled in comparison to this grim, reeking hole and the loss of so many raven lives. He refused to believe that Oelsa was among the dead.

A sharp snort came from the forest. He grabbed a thick branch from the ground.

Samson's fur lifted along his body as he hissed menacingly.

Another snort rumbled in the shadows, this one closer than the last. G.W. raised her wand, whispering words that set it sparking.

Branches snapped. The ground shook. Something immense pushed through the undergrowth.

G.W. lifted her wand, but before she could release the magic, a shiny head poked through the trees and stared out.

"Promelious?"

Promelious galloped forward, snorting and gargling. He skidded to a stop in front of G.W. and shook all over. His blades scissored back and forth, and the sun chose that moment to set them aflame. Promelious's face lit with joy.

"Oh, you beautiful beast," cried G.W. as she hurried to welcome him.

G.W. hoped their firelight would attract Fial and his raven troop. She listened for the familiar rush of wings to signal their arrival as the moon rose in the cold sky.

Near daybreak, an unfamiliar sound awoke them. Ardreas leapt to his feet. "Sounds like a wild animal thrashing through the underbrush."

Samson's whiskers twitched. "It's coming from over there."

A tall, tree-like creature burst into camp. The bare tree limbs were clutching a human, and the human was screaming. "Put me down, splinter head! Put me down!" The creature raced past them without slowing down.

"Did you see that? My eyes must be deceiving me." Ardreas scratched his head in disbelief.

G.W. stared as the stranger ran through the campfire. Its legs caught fire, and it plunged back into the woods leaving a flaming trail as the man's cries faded.

"Hurry!" G.W. cried. "They'll set the whole forest on fire!" She raised her wand and concentrated on bringing back the rain, but the fire exploded with a great roar. Flames leapt around the four companions. Grabbing her pack, G.W. shouted, "Run!"

Brand'oo sniffed the air and turned to Fial. "Smoke! To the west."

Fial winced at the acrid smell. "Our friends are in danger."

The raven troop swirled in a graceful wave of black motion and headed toward the fire.

Mangred finally found the tree soldiers frozen in place. He commanded them to drop the prisoner's log. "He's dead," Mangred said.

The tree soldiers stood mute, waiting for the next command.

Mangred tried not to think about the punishment for his failure. He sat on the log, head in his hands. "If I bring him the girl, I may at least escape with my life."

He reset the Hunt Disc rings. "What does she look like?" Mangred tried to imagine the girl, but he couldn't. The Disc remained inert. Mangred tried again and again. No picture formed in his mind. He failed four times. His panic grew. "I give up," he shouted as he threw the disc down.

Perhaps this was one of the Shadow Lord's last tricks, to teach his minion a lesson. Minutes ticked by when inexplicitly the Hunt Disc twirled its three rings and revealed to Mangred the direction in which he would find the girl.

"You tricky beggar," he laughed. He ordered the tree soldiers to pick up the prisoner's log. "We'll take it to the Master anyway. Maybe he'll know some spell to revive the dead."

Devastated by the certainty that Dahvi had died, Oelsa clung to his last message. "I'm sure you said I am the Key, but that doesn't make sense."

An intruder jabbed her mind.

"Ouch!"

Another jab.

"Shoo. Go away."

The jabs persisted.

"Leave me alone."

The voice was horribly familiar. "How delightful. I've found you." His laughter burst inside her head. Oelsa blanched.

"Weren't you waiting to hear from me?" His voice assaulted her.

"Go away. You have no right to be here."

Anvyartach's repugnant laugh grated against her mind.

"You killed him. And now you think I'm going to listen to you? Well, you're wrong. I don't have a Key, and even if I did, I wouldn't give it to you." Oelsa put every ounce of force she had into the last words. "So. *Get. Out!*"

Anvyartach had expected no resistance. "Stop that." He rubbed the glass orb vigorously and chanted the magic words. But he was too late. The connection with the girl was broken.

"You can't do that. I'm the Master." He shook the glass orb, wanting to see the one who dared defy him, but the glass was as muddy as the bottom of a river.

The evil presence left her mind like a door snapping shut. *I did that.* This victory buoyed her spirits and momentarily eased her grief. *I can think again.* She rubbed her forehead. *I can figure this out. I know keys unlock things and help solve problems.* Thoughts flowed more easily. *The first problem I need to solve is how to get that terrible voice out of my mind. Everything he says is a lie. All he wants is a key, and he's sure I have it. But he won't listen when I tell him I don't have a key. He frightens me so much.*

A long, buried memory surfaced. When she was very small, she found an ornate chest hidden under her father's bed. Inside, an old parchment covered in beautiful writing rested on a dark-blue, velvet cloth. It was the loveliest thing she ever saw.

The memory cheered her. When her father found her holding it, he took it from her and said she was too young to play with such a

precious gift. He gazed at it intently before he laid it back in the chest and locked it with a firm snap. The look on his face, Oelsa realized, had been full of love as well as pain.

The memory became clearer. She never thought about why her father and mother moved into the Heart of the Forest away from people, or why, after her mother died, her father didn't move back to civilization. Those decisions must be connected with that scroll.

Oelsa saw her solitary childhood in the forest in a new light. But if her father knew something about a Key, why didn't he tell her? He must have been waiting until she was old enough to understand. She gazed into the trees. Maybe it's such a terrible secret that he didn't want to burden her. But how could that beautiful scroll carry anything but light and joy?

A new voice spoke in her mind making Oelsa jump.

Listen to your heart, Oelsa. The Key is awake and you must use it wisely. Our world is depending on you.

Racing to escape the raging fire, G.W. concentrated on her grand-daughter Oelsa.

Listen, Oelsa—listen to the Key and its wise counsel.

35

"NOT SO FAST!" Mangred ran after the tree soldiers. "Slow down!" As the Hunt Disc pointed the way to the girl, they followed Mangred's orders with mindless obedience.

Thick smoke rose over Finnis Fews. Fial urged his troop to fly faster. "We've got to find the source of the fire before the smoke blocks our view. This is dark magic, Brand'oo. Can you feel it too?"

Brand'oo nodded and continued to fly.

"If the wizardess, her cat, and their rescued friend are caught in this, they don't stand a chance of escaping."

Fial thought about all the strange things that had happened recently. The girl had to be at the center of everything. The prophecy foretold it and Fial's visions were full of warnings. The Evil One from the First Time has returned and his power was growing. The evidence was overwhelming: the WilderOnes's encroachment into the forest, the deadly black ooze, the wizardess and her cat (both claiming to have had prophetic dreams), and the story of the wizardess's connection to the girl as well as to the Evil One. Now Finnis Fews was on fire.

"Hurry, Brand'oo. Time's running out."

Oelsa was growing more confused. Her father actually called her "the Key." It hurt to recall her father's dying words, but she had to know the truth.

She also had to know who was invading her thoughts demanding the Key. Why does he think it's his? How could she possibly steal something she knew nothing about?

"Ah, girl, you're opening up to me again. How delightful."

The Shadow Lord's voice dripped with insincerity and menace. "You don't need to be frightened of me, girl. I only want what's best for you, and what's best is for you to hand over the Key. We both know you have it, so just give it to me!"

"Stay away from me, you bully."

Anvyartach's laugh echoed again in her head.

"Why did you kidnap my father? He never did anything to you, and when he wouldn't give in to your demands, you killed him."

"Killed? I didn't kill anyone. How dare you accuse me of such a terrible thing. You should be more careful with your words, child." He jabbed a needle of pain into her head.

Oelsa winced but refused to give in. "Why are you doing this? You're mad."

"You're calling me names now? How quaint."

A shock of brilliant pain struck behind Oelsa's eyes.

"Did you never wonder why your father kept you so isolated there in the woods? Even when your mother left you?"

"My mother didn't leave me. She died."

Anvyartach was pleased the girl had risen so easily to the bait. "Oh, your mother had a choice. Who told you she died? Your father? Was there anyone else to corroborate his story? He could make up anything, and you'd have no way to tell if it was true or false."

"He wouldn't lie to me. I'm his daughter." A tiny worm of doubt wriggled into her mind. Could he have lied? Could her mother be out there, waiting to be found?

Anvyartach pressed harder. "Ah, hah! So you're thinking your father may not have been as truthful as you always assumed. He never told you about the Key, and that's the same as a lie. If he could lie about something like that—and this is a very big lie, girl—maybe he lied about other things as well . . ."

"Get out, you liar," Oelsa shouted. "You're trying to make me doubt things I know to be true, but it won't work."

Anvyartach shot a spark of pain into her left eye. "Oh, I'm having too much fun to leave just yet. Tell me, hasn't your life been exceptionally dull up to now? Just you and your father living there in the woods, all alone, with only animals to talk to? Safer that way, of course. Animals can't tell secrets."

"I'm not listening. Go away."

"Play time is over, girl. You have something that's mine. Tell me where you've hidden the Key."

Hungry, exhausted, furious, Oelsa ground out her words. "I'll tell you one more time. I do not have a Key, nor do I know anything about one. And even if I did, you're the last person I'd tell."

The words were barely out of her mouth when a fiery bolt of pain ripped through Oelsa's brain and to her stomach. "I do not have a Key!"

Anvyartach continued his brutal assault on the girl. "Give it to me, you wretched girl. It's mine."

Oelsa doubted she could endure the pain much longer. "Kill me, and you'll never know where it is."

The pain stopped. Oelsa caught her breath. "If you ever do that again, I promise you will never find your precious Key."

"Enjoy your breathing space, child, but don't think you've won anything. You'll soon give me the right answers."

Oelsa's stomach ached and her head throbbed. She tried to make sense of the nightmare engulfing her. *If I am carrying a Key,* she thought, *Father hid it too well. What do I do now?*

The facts hit her hard. Her father was dead and she no longer needed to rescue him.

A new smell pulled her from her thoughts. "Smoke? Is that smoke?"

The trees around her crackled as they caught fire. Terror shot through her. Oelsa scrambled over logs and patches of ferns into the inches-deep mat of dry pine needles—dry tinder that could burst into flame in an instant.

36

THE CONFLAGRATION RACED through Finnis Fews spurred by a powerful wind. The snapping and crackling of burning trees caused the friends to run harder. Ardreas stumbled over a root and sprawled in the loose duff. G.W. grabbed his arm and hauled him to his feet. "Okay?"

Fear stitched his side, but Ardreas nodded. Samson bolted ahead until the ground grew too hot. He leapt onto G.W.'s shoulder.

Behind them, Promelious lurched through the snarl of trees, barely ahead of the blaze. He wasn't built for speed. When G.W. saw him lagging too far behind, she worked a spell to protect him from the heat. She hummed tunelessly and faced Promelious who doggedly trudged after them.

> High and lo, wide and narrow,
> carry this beast straight as an arrow.
> Bring him safely through smoke and flame.
> Care for him 'til we meet again.

She hurled the spell. Their last image of Promelious was of incandescent magic surrounding his body.

From overhead, Fial saw the bright flash. "Down there, Brand'oo! It's them." He nearly wept at the sight of G.W. with Samson on her shoulder and Ardreas racing away from the forest's flames. He banked over G.W.'s head. "Follow us! There's an opening—not far!"

Their raven friends startled G.W. but relief spread through her. "Ardreas, pick up the pace!" Samson crouched against her shoulder, willing her to move like lightning.

The raven was difficult to see through the thick smoke, but Fial continued to urge them on. "Keep moving. There's a lake—might be big enough to stop the fire."

Samson dug his claws into G.W.'s cloak and crouched close to her neck until they splashed headlong into the lake. Ardreas sputtered and flailed in the cold water. G.W. muttered a spell for buoyancy. Samson added his feline magic to strengthen their swimming skills.

"Kick with your legs, Ardreas," G.W. shouted. "Arms in front—sweep the water behind you."

Fial called to his troop. "Quick! Find a way out of this!"

The three struggled through the water, their heavy clothes weighing them down. Seeing Ardreas tiring, Samson leapt into the water near him. "You're not going to give up, Ardreas. I'll tickle your chin and bite your ear if you even think about letting yourself sink."

Samson swam around Ardreas, nudging him with his head. G.W. grabbed hold of Ardreas's vest and pulled. "Keep going," she shouted. "The fire's almost to the shoreline. You can do this."

Fial and the ravens battled the intense drafts of heat rising from the forest. Their altitude gave them the advantage of seeing the fire's path.

"This way," Brand'oo called to Fial. "To the east."

Billows of smoke covered the lakeshore. Fial dropped close to the wizardess's head. "You're almost there. When you get to the other side, go right."

G.W. could barely see the far side of the water through the haze. "Samson, can you smell the far shore yet?"

Samson turned and swam steadily away from them.

"Follow the orange streak," G.W. shouted yanking Ardreas's arm.

Ardreas gasped and gulped another mouthful of water. But he kept moving.

The fire licked the edge of the lake. The water grew warmer.

G.W. could just make out Samson's orange fur as he leapt onto dry land.

Ardreas crawled out of the water and panted. G.W. hauled herself to her knees. "We did it!" she shouted. "Ride with me, Orange Light."

Samson raced to Ardreas and licked his forehead. "Told you I'd bite your ear if you gave up."

Smiling, Ardreas pushed to his feet and staggered after G.W.

Fial called from above. "Stay to your right. There's a rocky ridge not more than a hundred yards ahead. We'll wait there as long as we can."

When the fire reached the lake, the water steamed, quenching the leading flames. It might have quelled the flames completely if a sharp gust of wind hadn't carried sparks to the dried grasses beyond its edge. Fanned by the wind, the blaze flared and roared forward, devouring everything in its path.

The first rocks the three came to were the size of small animals, but these soon grew into boulders large enough to crush cottages. If they could reach the rocky peak rising above the forest floor before the fire caught them, they had a chance of survival.

Fire licked their feet as they climbed higher. A narrow path wound upward, wide enough for a mountain goat or a cat. One side dropped several hundred feet straight down. "Lean against the wall and don't look down," G.W. ordered Ardreas who wobbled near the edge.

Fial's troop called encouragement. Samson's claws had little grip on the rocky path, but with the ravens waiting above, he was determined to make it to the top. G.W. calmed her wildly beating heart and concentrated on moving upward. Ardreas inched after them, muttering, "Don't look down. Don't look down."

Slowly but steadily, they reached the top and sprawled on to the flat space. The ravens' carks and trills surrounded them.

The fire raged at the base of the rocky butte. The survivors were amazed by how completely the fire surrounded them. Their safety depended on clinging to the stony refuge above the fiery inferno.

"Glad we found you," Fial said as he set down beside G.W.

"It seems you and your clan have saved us yet again." G.W. bowed her head to him. "We are grateful, King of the Ravens."

Fial nodded.

The wizardess added, "Have you figured a way out of this hot spot?"

37

ANVYARTACH COMBED THROUGH his library of ancient books, seeking a way to force the girl to hand over the Key. "I know she has it." The angles in his face aligned like the slabs of granite forming the walls of his castle. "When I get my hands around her neck, I'll wring the truth from her!"

Running his bony fingers over the old books, he randomly pulled one out, then another and another. When none revealed the information he so desperately needed, Anvyartach threw them across the room. "Worthless."

He rested his head against a shelf and pounded his fist on top of it. "Worthless. Everything is worthless!"

Silently, the top of the shelf slid forward. The blow had dislodged a sticking hinge. Spellbound, Anvyartach watched as a small compartment lifted from within the shelf. He held his breath and poked a finger into it, probing every inch until he felt a tiny button on the bottom. When he pressed it, a second compartment opened.

"Oh, you beauty." He eased out a thin cloth from inside and set it on the table.

The cloth was edged in tiny scallops embroidered with gold threads and folded in thirds. Anvyartach lifted each fold revealing a delicate parchment, covered with ancient words. The ink had faded almost to invisibility. "Someone a long time ago didn't want anyone—meaning me—to know this secret."

Anvyartach lifted the wafer-thin parchment closer to his face. "This is written in the language of the First Creators when I, too, was one of them." A flood of dark memories hit him. "I've found your so-called prophecy. Its secrets will soon be mine, and then we'll see who has the real power in this world."

When Anvyartach attempted to read the ancient words, the script had faded, but the old language resonated in his memory, gradually revealing its meaning to him. Line by line, Anvyartach pieced the prophecy together.

"This is it," he whispered. "The secret is finally revealed."

The child will come from humble origins.
She will not know of the treasure she holds.
The treasure will be revealed only when a great need arises.
If she is not guided in the awakening of her treasure,
she will lose its power and never be able to regain it.
If a greater force appears before she understands
her power or how to use it,
that force may wrest the treasure from her.
Therefore, it is essential the girl must be told the secret
before . . .

His hand shook so violently he dropped the parchment and grabbed it up again. Reading the words a second and third time, he reveled in their meaning. "There is a Key . . . and the woodcutter's daughter has it. The stupid girl has the treasure and she doesn't know it." Dancing around the library, he giggled and kissed the parchment. "She's oblivious to the fact she has the Key, but even if she does know, she has no idea how to use it!"

Anvyartach clasped and unclasped his hands, giddy with the anticipation of holding the all-powerful golden Key in his palm.

As the fire raged through Finnis Fews, the FireIce rampaged underground. Animals fled for their lives, but their terror was too inconsequential to attract the crushing appetite of the black ooze. It craved something greater than simple animal fear. Somewhere near—it could feel this—was a huge reservoir of fear mixed with grief-stricken rage. The FireIce surged onward, driven by insatiable desire and a mad craving to devour every last drop of tantalizing, exquisite life energy.

"Mangred! Have you found the girl?"

"Master, the fire!" Mangred gasped in the smoke-filled air. "The fire is out of control. Why did you set it?"

"Fire? I didn't set any fire. Is it near the girl?" Anvyartach panicked. "Find her, Mangred, before it's too late!"

Mangred struggled to stand in front of the sprinting tree soldiers and yelled into the leader's face. "Stop!"

The entire phalanx of tree soldiers halted mid-step, surrounded by heavy smoke thickening around them.

"Master, I'm sure we're close to the girl. If we find her . . ." He swallowed. "I mean, *when* we find the girl, should the tree soldiers bring her back? They do know the way, don't they?"

A terrible thought struck Mangred: What if the Master had imbued Uhlak, and only Uhlak, with the directions for bringing the prisoner and the girl back?

Thinking quickly, Mangred said, "Master, don't worry. The girl can't be far. When I find her, I'll grab her and we'll race back to you. Right? Right. Trust me."

Inside, Mangred whimpered. This seemed so impossible.

Anvyartach's voice filled Mangred's head. "Oh, you *will* find her and bring her to me. Do not harm her. Not before I have what I need."

The tree soldiers stood frozen in place, waiting for Mangred's next command. Mangred raised his voice. "Listen up, you wretched stilts. There's a girl cowering somewhere near here. And we need to find her! Obey instantly, or you'll be feeding those flames licking at our heels!"

38

UNRELENTING HUNGER DROVE the FireIce toward the tantalizing well of raw emotions. When the FireIce burst through the ground into the forest, the intense heat blistered the ooze, evaporating it in seconds. Roaring with pain, it escaped below the surface. Frustration whipped the FireIce's frenzy for the vast source of life force just out of its reach, and hunger drove it deeper into madness.

The FireIce screamed as it raced. "MINEMINEMINEMINE!"

Smoke filled the forest until Oelsa could see no more than a few feet ahead. Grief bowed her shoulders. "You were so strong, Father. If only I had found you in time, I might have saved you." Oelsa struggled through the smoke. "If I had reached you in time, maybe this terrible monster in my mind would never have found me. He keeps dragging me closer to him no matter how much I resist."

She rested behind a mammoth cedar. A sliver of courage rose through her thoughts. "I've made it this far. I will find a way."

She straightened her shoulders, intending to push on, but the forest suddenly filled with crashing tree limbs and a man's angry shouts.

She peeked around the tree. The scene made no sense. A vast, grotesque army of trees was marching through the smoke.

She rubbed her eyes. Trees marching?

Rank after rank, like mindless puppets, these unnatural, deformed trees with their skeletal limbs hanging loosely at their sides lurched forward.

Oelsa watched a wild man leap from side to side in front of the first rank. He shook his fist, yelling at them, but the somber trees showed no reaction. They marched in mindless lockstep.

Oelsa backed away and fell over a gnarled tree root. "Oooff!" The word flew out before she could stifle it.

The man shouted. "Stop!"

The trees halted mid-step.

Mangred pointed towards Oelsa's hiding place. "There!"

Oelsa bolted from cover.

"Get her!"

Oelsa ran, dodging the thick tree limbs and hanging vines, pushing through clumps of bushes. The smoke helped hide her, but the racket she made gave her location away, and each time she glanced over her shoulder, they were closer.

Mangred roared, "Grab her! Grab her! Don't let her get away!"

Wild with panic, Oelsa failed to notice an unusual kind of energy expanding in her chest. As it grew stronger, and harder to ignore, an unexpected thought filled her mind: *So this is the mysterious Key.*

"At last! You're finally making sense, girl."

Oelsa stumbled as the detestable voice boomed into her head.

"Yes, this new sensation must be the Key. Don't fight it. Stop running and let my *friend* Mangred and his *helpers* guide you to me." Anvyartach's voice wheedled further into Oelsa's mind.

Oelsa felt the falseness of the words.

The man and the deformed trees encircled her.

"Don't be afraid. You can trust him. Honestly." The Shadow Lord's oily voice purred.

Mangred inched closer.

"My man means you no harm, girl. He just wants to talk to you."

Oelsa had seen the trees crush everything in their path. They represented something much more threatening than a man who simply wanted to talk. They would crush her if she got in their way.

Mangred bellowed, "Stand still, brat!"

Oelsa ran.

"Drop the log! After her!" Mangred's voice was like iron.

The prisoner's log thudded to the ground and the tree soldiers sprinted after Oelsa.

Watching the disaster through his glass orb, Anvyartach focused on Mangred. "Stop yelling at her, you imbecile. You're scaring her!"

"But she's getting away!"

"Don't shout. Be nice!" The last word choked Anvyartach.

Mangred shouted at Oelsa. "Wait! I . . . I promise I won't hurt you." The words were right, but the tone was as gruff and as threatening as before.

"Stay away from me!" Oelsa shouted over her shoulder. She slipped on wet leaves and went down on one knee. "Leave me alone."

Before Mangred could catch her arm, Oelsa twisted away and squeezed into a thicket of alders too dense for the large man to push through.

Panting to catch her breath, Oelsa prepared to flee when Anvyartach's voice filled her head. "Enough. He only wants to help you bring me the Key."

"Why should I do anything you say? I don't even know who you are!"

"Because if you don't bring me what is mine, and do it right now, you will end up like your father."

Rage fueled Oelsa's muscles. She plunged into the smoke-filled woods.

Anvyartach stroked the glass orb. His magic poured through it. His words grew stronger. They became a brilliant arrow of light that shot toward the fleeing girl.

"STOP!"

The crushing bolt struck Oelsa in the back. She staggered and crashed against an old hemlock lying on the forest floor. Stunned, she tried to will her legs to stand, but they wouldn't. She clawed at the ragged bark, pulling her body upward, dragging her useless legs behind her. With a grunt, she reached the top of the fallen trunk and gravity toppled her to the other side.

"Grab her, Mangred, while she's still stunned!"

Mangred commanded the tree soldiers to halt. They were useless as searchers. He leaned against the fallen hemlock and peered around it. "She's vanished. I can't see her anywhere."

"Right in front of you, numbskull. She can't go anywhere. She's paralyzed."

His Master's voice battered Mangred's mind. "Find her."

Oelsa smelled Mangred. He was close to her. She felt safe, hidden in a small, shadowy groove under the hemlock's trunk. She couldn't feel her legs. She willed her mind to go blank, trying to fool the fiend reading her thoughts.

"I know you're there, girl, and you can't move. Remember I can hear your thoughts." Anvyartach's intrusion tormented her.

She didn't reply.

"Show yourself, or you'll regret ever being born."

Anvyartach's threat seared her mind. She gasped.

Mangred heard her and leapt to his feet.

Feeling returned to Oelsa's legs like pins pricking into her flesh. She willed herself to stay still, but she was running out of options. *Think, think, think! How do I get out of this?*

Anvyartach shouted at Mangred. "She's right in front of you. I can hear her thinking!"

Mangred saw only the fallen hemlock. He grabbed a branch and scrambled up top. His eyes adjusted to its shadowy underside. "There you are." He jumped down and grabbed the girl.

He hauled Oelsa to her feet. He was about to throw her over his shoulder when he heard the roar of the wall of fire galloping toward them. The heat beat at Oelsa and Mangred. He bellowed. "Let's get out of here!"

Oelsa let Mangred grab her hand and pull her away from the terrifying fire. Inside her, the new sensation of the Key's presence grew stronger.

Mangred ordered the tree soldiers, "GO! GO! GO!"

They ran blindly. Mangred's grasp was the only thing that kept Oelsa upright and moving forward. A terrible odor came from the direction of the fire and Mangred hesitated.

"What's that stench?" Mangred didn't wait for an answer. He threw Oelsa over his shoulder and ran. As he veered to the left, the searing FireIce burst from the ground. Eyes bulging, Mangred heard Anvyartach screaming, but the words were a jumble.

Oelsa bucked against his hold. "Those things," she shouted. "They're moving straight for it!"

Mangred watched the tree soldiers march forward. One by one the stinking ooze incinerated every one of them.

"Protect the girl!" Anvyartach screamed.

The fire roared.

The maddened FireIce shrieked, "MINEMINEMINE!"

Mangred's grip slackened. He dropped Oelsa. The impenetrable wall of fire surrounded them. A monster from the bowels of the earth was devouring the ground on which they stood.

39

ON THE ROCKY SUMMIT, G.W. stiffened. "Oelsa. She's under attack. We have to rescue her, Fial."

"All I see are flames everywhere."

"She's in the middle of the inferno and there's something else—the black ooze. It's cornered her. Hurry, Fial, before it's too late. We'll follow."

The King of the Ravens leapt into the air, surrounded by an arrow of black wings pointing into the firestorm that was Finnis Fews.

Samson paced around G.W., his fur on end. "We'll be burned to a cinder the moment we leave these rocks."

Ardreas gripped his axe. "At home, we fought fire by creating a break it couldn't cross. I can cut a path wide enough to keep the fire at bay long enough for the two of you to run ahead of it."

"You would brave the flames for us?" G.W. asked. "You'll most likely be consumed before the first tree can be felled."

For an answer, Ardreas leapt over the edge and disappeared down the side of the mountain. They heard the ringing axe moments later.

G.W. looked at Samson, a smile spreading across her face. "He's doing it. Come on."

In moments, the wizardess and the orange cat followed him into the thick smoke. Below them, the inferno raged. As they neared the bottom of the rocks, a faint path opened into the blaze. The sound of the axe echoed just ahead of them.

Samson rode on G.W.'s shoulders. The heavy smoke made breathing nearly impossible. "How's he keeping ahead of these flames?" G.W. shouted to Samson. "Can you still hear the axe?"

"He's managing. The axe is still biting into trees—slower but steady."

"We need to help." G.W. straightened and lifted her arm. "Hear me, Grandmothers." As she drew a breath, she choked and doubled over coughing.

A strong hand grabbed her arm. "Can you keep moving?" Ardreas's face was red and his hair was singed. "Lean on me."

He tugged G.W. forward. "Stay put, cat. Your paws wouldn't last a minute in this fiery rubble."

Samson growled, not at Ardreas but at the horrendous inferno. "We can make it," he shouted at Ardreas. "Keep clearing the path, as long as you can." Samson's voice held no false hope that any of them would make it through this.

G.W. stepped away from Ardreas. "Go, friend. Do what you can. Samson and I can make it from here." She lifted her chin and nodded.

Ardreas smiled down at G.W., accepted her calm resolve, and hurried into the smoke. In moments, the axe's bite could be heard working through the flames.

From deep within G.W.'s being, the chant began to rise. Her hair drifted like a white halo around her head. She brandished her wand. With the voice of an eagle, G.W. commanded the fire. "MAKE A PATH THROUGH THIS INFERNO. LET US PASS!"

The flames wavered but did not subside.

Pulling her body upright, G.W. began another spell and gasped as a heavy smoke engulfed them. She staggered in the heat and bent forward. Samson clung to her shoulder, shouting encouragement.

G.W. marshaled her energy, lifted her wand, and leveled a deeper command. "Listen, inferno. I am daughter of Fionna, granddaughter of Ailis, descendant of Nuala L'Aege, the *first* to stop you from destroying the world!"

The flames trembled, pulled back from the path, and roared in protest.

Gasping, G.W. lifted her arm, and shouted, *"Make a path from here to the far place."*

G.W. pointed to the heart of the inferno, but before she could release the last word, she doubled over coughing.

Samson spoke into her ear. "You can do this."

Her body shook. She choked and dropped onto her knees, head down. Her energy was ebbing away.

Out of the smoke, blackened by the fire, the woodsman reached down, lifted the wizardess to her feet, put his arm around her shoulders, and coaxed her forward. "Come. A few more feet."

Stumbling, G.W. leaned against Ardreas. He guided her forward. Fire licked their steps, but the woodsman did not falter. "Hold on to me," he urged. "A little farther." His voice soothed G.W.'s uncertainty. She felt his strength and the ancient Grandmother magic rose within her.

From Ardreas's shoulder, Samson loosed his feline war cry.

"Awaken, Idelisia! Grandmother L'Aege and Samson of the Warrior Clan are calling you. Hear our command and rise!"

The fire shrieked and hovered just out of range.

His orange fur radiant in the fire's light, Samson renewed his demands. "You cannot resist our doubled powers, flames! We command you! Be gone!"

Samson's eyes blazed. His whiskers bristled like silver daggers and he cried again. "Consume yourself and die!"

Supported by Ardreas, G.W. and Samson commanded the roaring

inferno to shrink and flee from them. G.W.'s powerful Grandmothers magic grew. "Granddaughter Oelsa. Be strong. You have the gift of the Key. You must use the Key!"

The three companions ran.

Anvyartach pummeled Mangred's senses. "GRAB THE GIRL!"

His Master's voice pierced Mangred's jumbled thoughts. "But Master. The fire! The ooze! See how it's incinerating the tree soldiers! Tell me how to escape with her."

"Behind you, fool! Run while you can!"

Mangred grabbed for Oelsa, but she twisted away from his grip. The FireIce leapt toward her.

Drawn to the girl through Anvyartach's magic, the FireIce sang, "We will consume you! The Master wills it so!"

From his remote castle, Anvyartach bellowed. "THIS IS *NOT* MY WISH! Back away! BACK AWAY!"

The FireIce stalked closer to the girl.

"I COMMAND YOU! STOP WHERE YOU ARE! LEAVE THE GIRL ALONE!"

His words went unheeded. The FireIce had become its own master. This pulsing life energy would feed it forever. "MINEMINE-MINE!" the FireIce shrieked as it edged closer to Oelsa.

Mangred lunged for her. A dozen ravens led by Fial dove at him. They pulled his hair and pecked his arms. Mangred flailed trying to protect his head.

The flames surged forward and shot skyward. Smoke poured over the scorched earth. Blistering heat surrounded the man and the ravens.

Mangred saw Oelsa standing in the fire's path. "Move, girl! Run!" Velvet snapped.

Fial felt a heavy blow to his wing. "Retreat! The flames are too intense!"

The ravens lifted into the sky. Fial barely managed to keep up with them.

Mangred ran toward Oelsa. "You're coming with me."

Oelsa stared into the distance as though in a trance. Mangred yanked her arm and pulled her toward him. She fell, hit her head on a tree trunk, and slid closer to the edge of the FireIce.

"No you don't!" Mangred screamed, catching Oelsa's leg and heaving her away from the FireIce.

The FireIce leapt toward its prey. Mangred's eyes bulged. He grabbed the girl around her waist and fled deeper into the forest.

Every step was a battle. Mangred fought to escape the inferno and bring the Master his prize. In the mad dash, he tripped. Oelsa rolled free. The smoke thickened. Mangred couldn't see her. Gasping, he called out, "Master, the fire! If you want the girl, make a path for us!"

But Anvyartach's concentration was focused on the mighty force rising inside him. He clutched the orb and poured his darkest magic through it.

> Firestorm, oh, blackest heart,
> Created in the cauldron of vengeance
> Draw your flames away from this girl.
> Vast columns form, to imprison,
> not to harm her.
> Obey me now!

Mangred sprawled on the ground. He dared not look up to see what was happening. He felt the fire's heat. "NO! MASTER! Tell it to stop!"

The fire roared like a wild animal and raced forward.

Mangred cried out. "Run, girl!"

When he dared look, Mangred saw twenty-foot-tall columns of flame swirling and rising, encircling Oelsa who lay still on the ground.

Mangred raised his arm over his face and inched toward the fiery funnel. His skin burned. The heat singed his lungs.

"I can't reach her, Master! The fire—it's too hot. I've failed!"

Anvyartach ignored Mangred. He spoke to Oelsa. "You have no choice. These flames will never let you go. They obey my command only. If I say, 'Destroy the girl,' they will. And if I say, 'Bring her to me,' they will not hesitate to do so."

The voice was soft but menacing. Fear threatened to consume Oelsa. The flames grew hotter and hotter.

Outside the columns of fire, the FireIce raged. Still the fire blocked it. Desperate to consume this greatest source of raw emotions just out of its reach, the FireIce grew. Lifting into a seamless wave, the FireIce rose higher and higher, collecting its strength.

Oelsa pushed herself to her knees. The flame in her heart grew. "I am the Key. I am the Key."

She glowed red like a molten candle. "Awaken, Key!"

Head down, arms rigid at her sides, Oelsa chanted: "The Key awakens. *I* am awakening! *I am the Key!*"

Mangred watched the columns of flame encircle the girl. Desperate, he faced the inferno. "I will bring her to you, Master, if it's the last thing I do."

Holding Velvet over his head, Mangred pushed into the intense heat. Velvet snapped at the tongues of fire until its leather thongs were incinerated. Unheeding, Mangred whipped Velvet's handle. "Down, Fire! Dare not destroy what the Master desires!"

Flames scorched Mangred's arms and face. He fought his way closer to the girl. He did not see the FireIce before it vaporized him.

Gripping the glass orb, Anvyartach poured his energy into it. "Bring the Key Bearer to me!"

The fiery column encircling Oelsa rose higher. The FireIce engulfed the massive column. The fire screamed. Clouds of steam hissed. Heated gases exploded. A blinding white flash obscured it all.

40

THE EXPLOSION CONSUMED the FireIce above ground. The fiery columns encircling Oelsa rose higher.

As her power expanded, Oelsa's voice rose. "I am the Key of Idelisia."

Flames crackled around her. Heat pulsed.

Anvyartach held his breath.

Her words radiated strength and absolute authority.

Anvyartach's ancient forces flowed into his blood, electrifying his nerves. His tissues swelled with the ferocity from his first reign of terror. "I am Lord of the Dark Powers! The one and only Ruler of Idelisia! The Key belongs to me!"

He roared. "You cannot refuse! GIVE ME THE KEY!"

Oelsa's voice did not falter. "I am the Key. Your evil cannot persuade me, now or ever."

"You resist?" Anvyartach shouted. "Your father deserted you. Your mother abandoned you. No one can help you. The fire *will* consume you. Escape is impossible without my help. Give me the Key!"

Oelsa glowed. Her hair gleamed in the flame's orange and blue hues. She chanted the insistent words: "The Key has awakened. I am this Key. My strength has increased for millennia. I will save you, beloved Idelisia."

Flames licked closer.

Oelsa's voice rose over the crackling fire. "I am the Key. I am the Key."

Barbed lightning flew through the orb. It struck Oelsa's body. Bolt after bolt flew into her. She persisted. "Rise, Key. Fill me with your strength."

Anvyartach blasted her with more pain.

The trembling near Oelsa's heart increased. Energy thrummed through her body. Light expanded. The Key, buried for eons, had wrapped itself in layers of protection. The voice calling it now was an echo down an infinite tunnel.

The Shadow Lord poured his most corrosive magic into the glass orb. Green fire crackled within it. "Carry your malevolence to the child. Infect her mind. Destroy her spirit!"

The words thrilled Anvyartach. His sinister strength deepened. "You tried to destroy me, First Creators, but you failed! I will be *avenged!*"

The flames intensified.

The Evil One's words besieged Oelsa, but the Key's energy grew.

Anvyartach poured more and more dark magic into the orb. The orb glowed with blinding light. "Hear me, Idelisia, and weep! Only I will wield the Key!"

In the midst of the great furnace, Oelsa chanted the words in her heart. "The Key is awakened! I will save you, Idelisia!"

FireIce erupted beneath her feet. Its stench choked Oelsa. Flames reached higher and higher.

"I am the Key!"

Oelsa disappeared into the flames.

41

FLAMES THREATENED THEM. G.W.'s wand wove through the blistering air. Samson shrieked age-old, feline magic. Racing ahead, Ardreas pushed against the heat. An impenetrable tower of whirling flames blocked their path.

"What is that?" Ardreas shouted.

Head down, focused on quelling the flames, G.W. and Samson ran into his back.

Samson flew into Ardreas's chest, his claws extended to slow his fall. Ardreas grabbed him and caught G.W.'s shoulder before she collapsed. The three friends stared at the blazing whirlwind of fire.

G.W.'s sudden cry pierced the air. "It's surrounding Oelsa! The Evil One has entombed her within this fire!"

The old magics intensified and coursed through her. "Hear me, Grandmothers! The Key Bearer is in danger! Set her free!"

Samson bristled in Ardreas's arm. "Set me down, friend. We fight to the death."

Ardreas stood, legs apart, axe in both hands. "Until my last breath, cat. I stand beside you."

G.W.'s body was incandescent. Samson's rugged powers buffered them against the inferno. Flames of Finnis Fews licked around them while columns of fire encircled the girl who was the Key.

Anvyartach's words were spikes thrust into Oelsa's heart. "You have lost this game, girl. Give up. Give me the Key!"

"You are only shadow," Oelsa said. "You will bend your knee to me. I am the Key of Idelisia."

"Bow to you? These flames will consume you. The FireIce is maddened by its desire to consume you. You have no power!"

The flames drew closer. The FireIce howled.

Radiant light enveloped Oelsa. "I am the Key. Do with me as you will," she called to the universe as she disappeared.

"The Key is mine!" Anvyartach's triumph exploded from him. "It's there, in the ashes. I will reign forever!"

Anvyartach swept from the hall. His dark cape swirled around him. "All I need is the spell to reveal where the Key has fallen and Idelisia is mine!"

The words thrilled him. Anvyartach reached inside his cloak for the glass orb.

He set the orb on the table. Shocked, he shook the glass violently. "But you just channeled my power through you. You can't be"—he choked—"empty."

He stared at the cold object and screamed. "Where are her ashes? Show me the Key."

Eyes blazing, Anvyartach trampled the books strewn across the floor. He wrenched the shelf with the hidden compartment from the wall and thrust his hand inside. "There's more here. Show me!" He groped for something, anything, to guide him to the Key.

"Empty!" He hurled the shelf across the room.

Anvyartach fell to his knees and clawed through the crumbling parchment pages. His mouth stiffened in a rictus of fear. He trembled uncontrollably as wave after wave of disbelief rolled through him. The loss of Mangred and Uhlak, the destruction of the first squad of tree soldiers, the FireIce's dissolution, coupled with the glass orb's lost powers crushed him.

"The Key. You have to be there in the ashes. Reveal yourself." Anvyartach howled in defeat.

42

RADIANT IN THE LIGHT, Oelsa cried, "The Key is awake." Flames kissed her face. The Key softened their frenzied adoration.

With each breath, Oelsa repeated, "I am the Key." She lifted her hands toward the column of fire. The flames sighed. They bowed in reverence. And died.

At her feet, the FireIce trembled.

"Hear me, foul thing. You will never threaten our world again." Oelsa pointed at the poison. It shriveled to powder and blew away.

She walked to the edge where the flames had imprisoned her. Her friends were huddled together, charred and unmoving. "Ah, Grandmother, your knees will be stiff if you don't rise." She touched G.W.'s shoulder. Color returned to the wizardess's cheeks.

"Good Ardreas, your back must be painful from being arched so protectively over these two. Let your muscles ease." She leaned over her friend and whispered the words that had risen inside her while engulfed in the flames. "Rise, dear friends. We have much work to do."

Oelsa reached for Samson. He gingerly shook his hind leg and attempted to move from the wizardess's side.

"Poor cat. Most of your hair is singed off. Your whiskers are curled back . . . and your tail. Poor tail, bent at such an awkward angle." Oelsa gently stroked his side.

Samson gazed at the radiant girl. "What a sorry sight we must be. No way to greet our new friend."

Oelsa's healing energy surrounded her in waves, warming the cat and quelling the residual terror left from the fiery battle.

Ardreas sat up carefully. "You look different, Oelsa. Fire can transform a girl, I see." It hurt to laugh, but he beamed at the girl.

"It seems you have rescued us again, woodsman. Thank you for protecting my grandmother and her noble cat."

G.W. remained on the ground. Ardreas gently lifted her into his arms. "Where can we take her that will be safe, Oelsa?"

"Here, my friend. Let me look at her." Oelsa touched her grandmother's cheek and whispered words Ardreas could not hear.

Slowly G.W. opened her eyes. "So, Ardreas, you've relinquished your axe for a greater burden," she said patting his arm. "What would we have done without you, brave friend?"

G.W. studied the small group. "My child. We thought we'd never find you." She took Oelsa's hand and held it to her heart. "You are the Key, dear one. You know this, don't you? How you have been tried."

G.W.'s kindness and love encircled Oelsa and cheered her.

"The Key has found its rightful place. We have much to talk about, child."

"I have so many questions, Grandmother."

G.W. grasped Oelsa's hands, their heads bent toward each other. "All the years we have been apart, I knew you were out there, Oelsa. I sensed your existence, and now I wish to know everything about you as well."

Their conversation was interrupted by a wild cry from overhead.

"*Cark! Cark! K-K-K-K-K!*" Trills and whistles rang around them as the raven troop dropped into their midst.

"Fial, you rascal. You've found us." G.W. leapt to her feet. "I thought . . ." She couldn't finish the terrible thought of what might have happened to the ravens. She wiped tears from her eyes.

The King of the Ravens swept his great wings out to his sides, whirled, and shape-shifted into the magnificent magician. "What a miracle," Fial said. "The last we knew, you were about to be roasted in that column of fire." He embraced G.W. carefully, nodded to the bedraggled Samson, and shook Ardreas's hand.

Fial turned to the girl sitting next to G.W. "Oelsa?" She must be the same girl he'd found in the Heart of the Woods, but she was no longer a small, frightened child. Radiant light suffused her.

The Raven King dropped to his knee. He and the rest of the ragged raven troop bowed to her.

"Please rise, Fial. All of you," Oelsa said. "If I'm not mistaken, you tried to stop that dreadful man who wanted to harm me. Such bravery. I can never thank you enough."

"I thought you were lost forever," Fial said. "But here you are, vibrant with Idelisia's Key. It is we who are in your debt."

The raven clan ruffled their neck feathers and clacked their beaks in their highest praise.

"This isn't the only miracle," Fial announced with a sweeping gesture. "Look who else we found."

The lost Biab hopped to Samson and gently patted his head with her wing. "Thought the next time we met you were going to show me some new tricks, cat, or should I say Scraggly Paws?"

"Don't worry, Feather Bait. There's plenty of time for new tricks." Samson purred, and butted his head against Biab's side.

The bedraggled group camped in a charred patch of Finnis Fews. In the morning, the ashen sky reflected their surroundings. Each stirred, still exhausted from the fiery battle with the Shadow Lord.

Samson rubbed G.W.'s outstretched hand. "How are you, old friend? You were magnificent, by the way."

G.W. sat up and tickled Samson under his chin. "How is Ardreas this morning? Without him and his axe, I'm not sure we would have made it through those flames."

Ardreas relaxed close to them, awed again by Fial's transformation from raven to magician.

"Not many would have walked into that maelstrom, Ardreas," said Fial. "You not only opened a path for G.W. and Samson, but you brought them safely through it. These are the actions of a true hero, my friend." The raven clan set up a loud chorus of approving *cark-cark-cark-k-k-k-s*.

"No more than all of you," Ardreas said, his face reddened from the praise.

Oelsa sat next to her grandmother and leaned against her. "Thank you for coming to my rescue. I felt your powers strengthening me, even though I had no idea from where they were coming."

"The power of the Key awakened in you, Oelsa," G.W. said. "Without you and your Key, I hate to think what our fate might have been." She put her arm around Oelsa and drew her into an embrace. "So much is new, you must feel such confusion."

Oelsa allowed herself to be comforted. It had been a long time since she had felt such a loving embrace. "When the Key awakened inside me," she said, "the sensation was almost indescribable. Power, love, justice, all mixed with a sense of overwhelming joy." A soft light radiated from her face and body. "But I have no idea how to call it forth or how to control it. Will I ever understand?"

Samson butted his head against Oelsa's leg and purred. "You are stronger than you realize, Key Bearer." Despite several scorched patches in his orange fur, Samson stood regally. "Of course you will. But we don't have time to waste. Anvyartach may be defeated at the moment, but he's very much alive. Failing to grab the Key will only goad him to seek revenge and who knows what new, harsh steps he'll take."

"Yes, Orange One, I can feel his malevolence even from a distance," G.W. said. "He will not give up until he gets what he wants.

And he wants Oelsa's power so he can punish Idelisia for his banishment. We've bought some time for now."

Oelsa paled at G.W.'s words. The birth of the Key had demanded more than anything she had ever experienced, and the challenges had only begun. "I feel as though I might sleep for days," Oelsa said, "but there's no time."

"First things first, child," G.W. said. "Samson and I will help you find—"

Something big crashed through the singed trees. An eerie gargling noise grew louder. Snorting and puffing, a silvery creature burst into the clearing.

"Promelious?" G.W. said as she hurried forward.

The scissory beast who had once tried to eat Ardreas and been saved by G.W.'s kind heart stood among them. "Yes, it is I, the one you rescued a second time with your magic, Grammy Wizard L'Aege." He bowed to her. "You could have left me to die in the flames, but you didn't. Your spell gave me the strength to stay ahead of the fire until I made it to safety."

G.W. threw her arms around Promelious's neck and wept with relief. Standing back, she said, "I sense a change in you, Silver One."

Oelsa approached and laid her hands along his back. "I feel this too. You are not what you first appeared to be, are you?" She leaned closer to Promelious's side and listened to his heart. "You are something else entirely."

The Key's awakening power flowed from her core, down her arms, and into the silvery scissors on Promelious's body. "You were something else entirely before those wicked beetles worked their black magic against you, someone quite different."

The creature shimmered under Oelsa's touch. As she chanted words of transformation, a glinting river of light poured over Promelious.

A thunderous clap knocked all of them to the ground.

When they staggered to their feet, a splendid silver-winged horse stood where the scissory beast had been. "My true form," Promelious said, "before the beetles captured me."

He nodded to G.W. "Your goodness saved me, wizardess, and your granddaughter has set me free. I am here to repay your gift." He nuzzled her white hair.

G.W. patted Promelious's head. The smile that spread from her mouth to her eyes crinkled well-worn wrinkles across her face. "What an amazing creature you are."

Promelious stepped back and flexed his powerful wings. They stretched ten feet from tip to tip, and their thick feathers were tinged with gold. His coat was a soft gray, like a wild rabbit's fur, and his mane and tail curled in long silvery waves. Each of his four hooves glinted with pearlescent chips of light that sparked with every step. He stood more than sixty inches at his shoulders and his powerful muscles shivered with anticipation. A silver star graced his forehead and his deep, lavender eyes were like velvet. Promelious was magnificent.

He turned his gaze on Oelsa. "My mission is to take you to a safe and secret place, Key Bearer."

She stared at him.

"According to the Prophecy a beast with silvery wings will take the Key Bearer—that's you, isn't it?—to a place of safety where she can regain her strength and learn to use her new powers. I know a place where the Shadow Lord will never find you."

"I don't recall this part of the Prophecy, Promelious," G.W. said. "Yet it makes sense to protect our fledgling Key Bearer."

Ardreas stepped toward Oelsa and touched her arm. "Are you comfortable with this?" He kept his eyes on Promelious as he spoke into her ear. "We don't really know him." Despite the current appearance, Ardreas still remembered the Promelious he first encountered in the beetles' cave.

"Thank you for your concern, Ardreas, but I have seen into his heart and am sure of his loyalty." She turned and her knees buckled.

Ardreas caught her before she could fall.

"I am weaker than I imagined, friend. The winged one's offer is more appealing with every minute," Oelsa whispered.

G.W. and Samson hurried to Oelsa. "Rest and gather your strength, Oelsa," G.W. said. "You will be tested again, and the next time the threat will be greater. Now that Anvyartach has tasted the Key's powers, he will crave it more than ever. He too must rebuild his strength and weapons. The FireIce may seem like a toy compared to his next creations." Certainty weighed every word.

"The battle is won, but this war for dominion over our beautiful land is far from over." Promelious smiled at G.W. and turned to Ardreas. "Place her on my back, Ardreas. It is time for us to be away."

Ardreas hesitated until Oelsa nodded assent. He picked her up and turned toward her grandmother.

G.W. stepped toward them and lightly kissed Oelsa on the cheek. "Until we meet again, dear one. Promelious will take good care for you. Trust him. Our love is with you always."

Samson's assuring purr reached up to her.

Fial took her hand and kissed it. "Until you need us, Key Bearer."

Biab, Brand'oo, and the raven troop's deep *prruk-prruk-prruks* echoed in loud salute.

Solemnly, Ardreas placed Oelsa on to Promelious's back, where she nestled between his wings.

Promelious bowed to the gathering, took a few steps, and rose majestically into the air on giant, silver wings. "The Key Bearer will be safe until Idelisia calls."

Acknowledgments

When I left teaching, for the second time, I was eager to try something new. *Why not write a novel?* I thought. *How hard can it be?*

Discovering the answer to this question has been a long and adventurous journey, filled with amazing people. I wish to thank all these friends, both old and new, who have shared their knowledge, encouragement, and unfailing support throughout.

Thank you Sarah Miner at Bookmobile, for expertly guiding the book through the publication process. Sarah is creative, smart, professional, unflappable, and exactly the right person for this first publication experience. I can't thank you enough, Sarah! All the people at Bookmobile have been wonderful. Thank you also to Mark Jung and the folks at Itasca Books for their help with the distribution of the book. My book has been in truly great hands.

I've also had the *best* editors working with me throughout this journey. Thank you Cathryn Ingolfsrud Jarvis, for being brave enough to edit the first draft of this manuscript. This was not an easy task, but you taught me so much about good writing. You were tough and kind and always encouraging. Thank you, dear friend!

Mary Logue, your words of support surprised and delighted me. After critiquing an early version of the book, you told me, "You're one of us now." Thank you for believing in the story and in my ability to bring it to life.

Samantha Parsons, my sweet, young pen pal, when you suggested we write a book together, it sounded like such fun. Your enthusiasm convinced me to start writing this story and inspired me to keep going. Your superb editing skills on the second draft were amazing as well. You also inspired the name of one of the key characters!

Larry Mellman, your understanding of story structure is flawless. Your ability to see the essential elements of the story has guided me through draft after draft. What a generous and tireless editor you have been. Guardian angel you are.

My extraordinary writers group has shared their wisdom and support throughout the writing of this story. Ann Kraemer, Kathy Zappa, Melissa Black, Kathleen Melin, Larry Mellman, and Kris Heim, your wise and gentle guidance and wholehearted encouragement have taught me *so much*. I love you all!

My wise and wonderful nieces Leila and Sadie Lowry and my astonishing granddaughters Elspeth and Onnee Roe have all inspired the character of O (Onnee) - E (Elspeth) - L (Leila) - SA (Sadie)! Each of you brings such joy, love, and creativity into the world! You are the lights of my life. Thanks to your great parents as well—Marcus Lowry and Shannon Pergament, and Quillan and Kim Roe.

Thank you to numerous fifth grade FOCUS students at Robbinsdale, ISD 281, elementary schools (2011–2017), for your enthusiasm for the story as well as for suggesting the title of this book. Thank you to your amazing teachers, Melissa Hood, Susan Beaubaire, Kim Boursier, Jennifer Weinand, Julie Hjerpe, and Sarah Prindeville, who welcomed me into your classrooms and let me write stories and poems with your marvelously creative students.

Thank you to all the readers of an early version of the story and for their great feedback: Brynn DeVaan (with grandmother Gretchen Valdez), Saya Slettehaugh (with grandmother Sharon Slettehaugh), Taliesin Montello (with Chris Lowry), and Sadie and Leila Lowry (with Mom Shannon Pergament and Dad Marcus Lowry). Thanks to Marcus also for so generously offering the use of his library, Moundsview Public Library, for my publication reading as well as writing the book's first review on short notice. Blessed nephew.

Thank you Sue Booth-Forbes, for providing Anam Cara, an Artist and Writers Retreat located on the Beara Peninsula in western Ireland. This was a dream come true. The warm and welcoming Irish folks, the sea, the mountains, the tree-lined narrow lanes, the O'Sullivan castle ruins, the ubiquitous sheep, and the many women who were also staying with you—it all touched a deep place inside me. Your friendship, the amazing conversations around the kitchen table, your excellent editing advice, the incredible food, oh my—you contributed much needed support to my burgeoning self-confidence as a writer. Thank you for those three amazing weeks!

Thank you Gretchen and Carl Valdez, for opening La Lomita in Espanola, NM, to my family and me so many times. Your home overflows with love and peace, ready acceptance of all who enter, and a deep spiritual presence that fills every inch. Inspiration was everywhere—Black Mesa, hummingbirds hovering along the *portal*, tai chi in the desert, New Mexican cuisine (HOT), and the many friends you have made there. I am so grateful for your love and support over the years.

I've been blessed to have many, many friends who have believed in me and my ability to create this story, no matter how long it has taken. Thank you from the bottom of my heart to each and every one of you!

Special thanks to two wonderful writers who were also extraordinary teachers. They said, "Yes, you can!" when my courage faltered. I feel such deep gratitude to you, Deborah Keenan and Michael Dennis Browne.

Thank you Tracy Thomas Wilson, for reading early versions and giving such great feedback. So generous. So perceptive!

Thank you Brooke Dierkheising of "Hoot Your Words!," for much needed guidance into the world of self-publishing, as well as to Amy Egenberger, for your life coaching and for leading those wonderful workshops.

My amazing, talented, kind-hearted, generous son Quillan Hunter Roe has created incredible illustrations and the cover illustration. Your vision has captured the essence of the characters and actions perfectly! Working with you on this project has filled my heart with such love and thanksgiving for the blessing you are in my life, sweet son.

My deepest thanks goes to my beloved husband Stephen E. Roe.

I could never have done this without your unfailing love and support. Who else would travel to so many faraway places for inspiration and spend days patiently waiting while I wrote and wrote and wrote? You've been my first and best editor and story shaper, and the fountain of infinite belief in me. Thank you, sweet *Gamache*. (And thank you Louise Penny, for seeing this as his true nature as well.)

About the Author

SHARON A. ROE lives in paradise, a.k.a. Kirkwood Hollow, in Plymouth, MN, in her multigenerational home with her amazing husband Stephen, her beloved musician-and-artist son Quillan, her equally talented and beloved daughter-of-the-heart Kim, and her two creative, curious, and adorable granddaughters Elspeth and Onnee.

Sharon's early years were spent daydreaming in a small town in southeastern Iowa, plotting her escape to the "Great World Out There." After a summer waitressing at Bob's Clam Shack in Gloucester, MA—where she lost her heart to the exotic New England landscape and the artists colony where she lived in a cold water flat over the harbor—she returned to Iowa to finish college, and met her True Love. (He had just arrived from a long, hot, and baffling road trip "Way Out West," i.e. from beautiful Ithaca, NY, to Iowa City, IA. Who wouldn't fall in love with a boy from "Out East" who lived in his 1955 Ford station wagon?!)

Although Sharon swore she'd *never* be a teacher, after a year as the World's Worst Secretary Ever, she reconsidered. She found a job teaching Language Arts to seventh graders and discovered she not only could teach, but she actually loved it. After half a century living in the land of Paul Bunyan and walleye fever and a quarter of a century teaching, she still loves writing and working with children.

Sharon A. Roe has been writing seriously for umpteen years—poetry, memoir, and the novel. Inspired by beloved poet and teacher Deborah Keenan's words that "all who write are feeding the Great River of Story," Sharon has made her first contribution to that river, Book One of *The Key of Idelisia* trilogy.

Left to right: Elspeth, Quillan, and Onnee

About the Illustrators

ELSPETH A. ROE is ten years old. She can be cute and calm sometimes, but wild and crazy at other times. She loves drawing, music, dance, running, reading, and math. When she's not at school, she's either playing outside, riding her new red, big-girl bike, or doing crafts. Her favorite color is red, and her favorite books are *Harry Potter*. She gets her art talents from her dad. When she's an adult, she plans to be in a bluegrass band, following in her parents' footsteps.

ONNEE R. ROE is eight years old. She *loves* playing outside, both in winter and summer. When she's not outside, she loves to play with magnet tiles; do crafts; make origami boats, cranes, or fish; and she's always looking for new patterns. She *loves* robots and swimming. She's been reading since she was four, and her favorite book so far is *Moo* by Sharon Creech. When Onnee is an adult, she wants to be a veterinarian because she loves all animals.

QUILLAN H. ROE is the co-creator of the Roe Family Singers, a great old-time, bluegrass, and gospel music group. He plays banjo, guitar, and upright bass, and writes many of the songs they perform. When not playing music, he loves drawing with his daughters, making posters for the band, having family hugs, and being a great dad and husband. Quillan has been creative all his life, writing his first book when he was four and drawing pictures since he could hold a pencil. He lives in Kirkwood Hollow with his beautiful wife Kim, and his two curious, creative and brave daughters Elspeth and Onnee.